D0570986

Willie Morris

After All,

It's Only a Game

WITH ART BY
Lynn Green Root

University Press of Mississippi   Jackson and London

Author and Artist Series

Copyright © 1992 by the University Press of Mississippi
Text copyright © by Willie Morris
All rights reserved

95 94 93 92   4 3 2 1

"The Phantom of Yazoo" is an excerpt from *North Toward Home* (Houghton Mifflin, 1969). "Me and Ollie" is from *Good Old Boy and the Witch of Yazoo* (Yoknapatawpha Press, 1989). "Cheerleaders vs. Baton Twirlers" is from *The Courting of Marcus Dupree* (Doubleday, 1983). "The Fumble" first appeared in *Always Stand in Against the Curve* (Yoknapatawpha Press, 1983).

Printed in Hong Kong by Everbest Printing Co., Ltd.

Library of Congress Cataloging-in-Publication Data appear on page 96.

C O N T E N T S

To Gibson, Graham,
Jay, Sara, and Bae

—after all, it's only a new family

FOREWORD

The day began as one you live for, a breezy autumn football Saturday. Willie Morris's beloved Ole Miss Rebels were playing, as Willie called them, "those loathsome Tennessee Volunteers" at Vaught-Hemingway Stadium in Oxford. Willie admires Tennessee's coach Johnny Majors, who is his friend, but any team Ole Miss plays is, for that one Saturday, loathsome. It was a celebrative weekend, anyway. The night before, Oxford had hosted the world premiere of the Disney movie made of Willie's classic children's book, *Good Old Boy*.

Before the game we gathered at Willie's place on campus for fried chicken, biscuits, Bloody Marys, and grave discussion of the afternoon's grand event. The afternoon held such promise that the foreboding weather report was largely ignored. I departed for the press box, much in envy of the rest of the party who headed to the south end zone for a considerably more partisan view.

Dog Brewer's Ole Miss Rebels took an early lead, delighting the festive home crowd. But at halftime while the bands played and the home crowd celebrated, heavy, dark clouds rolled in from the north and west. This was before the Ole Miss stadium had lights, and when the teams came back on the field, mid-afternoon had grown dark and evil.

I still don't know which hit with more force in the second half, the storm or Tennessee. High winds arrived first. Then rain. It rained so hard we could scarcely see the field from the press box. The mud-covered players became indistinguishable. We could see that most of what happened took place near the Ole Miss goal line. And we could see that the Tennessee scoreboard numbers kept changing, while the Ole Miss numbers stayed the same. Frankly, God's own light show of streaks and bolts had captured most of my attention. By the end of the third quarter, the stands were nearly empty. From the press box, we could see hail bouncing off the metal bleachers.

Late in the fourth quarter, the issue long decided, I turned my binoculars to the south end zone stand. There, huddled under one tiny umbrella, were Willie Morris and my wife Liz, the only two who remained. I was astonished. As the final seconds ticked down and Tennessee players celebrated, I went by the south end zone on the way to do interviews in the locker rooms. "What in the world are y'all doing still here?" I asked.

Willie, his eyes still fixed on the game, never changed his somber expression.

"Waiting for snow," he answered.

He then took from his soaked pants his soaked wallet, removed a soggy twenty-dollar bill, and said, "Twenty dollars for anything dry."

I tell this story for a couple of reasons. One, it shows Willie's love for the game. Two, it shows my friend's wonderful sense of humor. (My wife later told me that during the worst of the storm, Willie pointed to the Tennessee bench where the Volunteers were wearing orange rain slickers over their uniforms. "Look," Willie said, "the Ole Miss Rebels are playing the Tennessee Highway Department.")

The stories about football, baseball, and basketball that follow show eloquently the same love and devotion to sports and the same wonderfully keen sense of humor. And they also show an unmistakable understanding of the essence of sports and the emotions our games evoke. In a serious moment, Willie has confided, "Sports were so much a part of my growing up, of my becoming a man, that they are now a part of me."

It is that way for so many of us. For what are sports if not a metaphor for life? In sports, we learn to play with pain. In life, we work, despite debilitation, to do what is necessary. Anyone who competes to any extent inevitably fumbles a football or kicks a groundball to lose the big game. In life, despite our best, most earnest efforts, we sometimes fail. In both we must deal with success and failure, with incredibly wide-ranging emotions, and with self-esteem that can rise and fall like a river. In sports, it can all happen in a matter of seconds—and there's no place to hide.

In "The Blood Blister" Willie's protagonist endures a profane and demanding coach—didn't we all?—and so much more. At one point, he asks in retrospect, "Why did I love the game so much?"

Willie Morris knows. And his words and stories make us love the games all the more.

Rick Cleveland

PREFACE

My Father and Sports

When I was twelve years old my father gave me a small second-hand portable Smith-Corona for Christmas. I don't know why he gave me a typewriter then. Surely he didn't know I would be a writer someday, nor of course did I. But he did know I loved sports and wanted to write about them for *The Yazoo Herald*, which I subsequently did at age thirteen, reporting Yazoo City vs. Satartia and Yazoo City vs. Belzoni baseball games for Mr. Norman Mott, Sr., of the old *Herald*, in one baseball account quoting Keats's "Ode on a Grecian Urn," which Mr. Mott said he would tolerate if I could just provide the final score next time, since I had failed to do so in the first game I covered.

The little Smith-Corona later served me nobly as editor of *The Yazoo High Flashlight*, pecking away on it with two fingers as I did, at a minuscule yellow desk in my bedroom, about school spirit and cheerleaders and majorettes and dances entertained by a black Mississippi ensemble called The Red Tops, and after that when I went far away to college in Texas and continued for a time to write about sports. I carried the Corona to England when I attended school there and wrote my father on it about rugby and cricket.

In the months before he died, my father wrote me once a week in England on his big office manual in the Goyer Wholesale Grocery Company. Most of his letters were about sports, about how the Yazoo Indians were doing against Belzoni or Indianola or my alma mater, the Texas Longhorns, against the loathsome Aggies or Ole Miss vs. Mississippi State, but I see now they were really letters of love.

By accident I came across the old Smith-Corona not long ago, all derelict and rusty, in a forlorn crate containing the mementos and artifacts of my boyhood days. The words that came from it, and the other typewriters that followed, have caused me a lot of pain and questioning beyond sports, but I'm still glad Daddy gave it to me.

W. M.

Basketball

The Blood Blister

FICTION

is motivated by two things," Asphalt Thomas was wont to say—"reward and fear." Late afternoons were for basketball practice, and two nights a week for the games.

He harangued us unmercifully in the practices. "You're the puniest excuse I ever *seen* for ballplayers," he would shout, after some special miscue. "Start hustlin' or I'll put somethin' on you Moses couldn't get off. You couldn't whup the little girls' team at the Ursiline Convent. Keep your eyes open, dammit. A man can observe a whole lot by just watchin'." Then, a little further into the scrimmage, morose and growling, his whistle hanging disconsolately from his bullish neck, he would say, "Noggin, what the hell's wrong with your scrawny ass? I don't appreciate them black circles under your eyes. What time you get in last night?"

" 'Bout eleven, I think."

"Yeah? Hong Kong time? Get your pitiful tail off the court. I'm gonna play a little with these other turds." Using his long thorny elbows as he played, he would smack skulls, noses, ears, midriffs, making buffoons of his sullen charges with his deft Southeastern Conference moves and fakes and shots, leaving us prone on the floor in his imperious wake. After his fifth straight basket he would say, "I'm hotter than a depot stove," and then he would have us circle the arena twenty-five times around with his sadistic windsprints, and order Leon the manager to guard the water fountain in the locker room afterwards.

During the games I sat at the end of the bench and, like a neglected and forgotten sophomore gosling, more or less languished there. Because of the injuries there were only nine boys on the team, almost all of them seniors, but Asphalt Thomas would sometimes look down my way where I crouched numb and fetus-like to avoid his attention. One was not at all unproud in those days of the crimson knee-guards and the heavy crimson warm-up suits with "F.L." in white over the Number 18 on the back, but what in the world was I doing there? Why did I love the game so much?

Soon in high school there would also be some football and baseball, but there was something about this game that especially attracted and excited me, some soaring sense of beauty and accomplishment and adventure and even mischief to it, that when you wanted to you could play it all by yourself, and use your imagination on your own private fantasies. I was forever whipping the loathsome, arrogant Kentucky Wildcats on twenty-footers at the buzzer. And it was *fun*, putting the ball into the hoop, and then the melodic whish of the net strings when it was true—it was the sound of the *whish* above all that mattered so much. Not long before he died my father had put up a goal for me in our backyard when I was hardly tall enough to get the ball to the rim, but over the years my solitary practices in all climates and seasons, once or twice even in the *snow* when the net itself was frozen solid, had earned me my place on the varsity. It seemed a long time ago that I first started coming out here in the yard, alone, shooting the ball through the lonesome moments until it was too dark to see the hoop or the ball against the sky, succumbing to the lazy thoughts and daydreams, a formless rite of solitude, trying to figure things out a little, about trying to grow up, I guess, and over time the bouncing ball and my own footfalls had worn away the grass, so that the ground around the goal was spare and hard and useful.

Travelling to our away games on the feeble crimson-and-white sports bus with "The Choctaw" emblazoned on its sides, we would watch the nocturnal prospects drift past, the dark expansive flatland with its row after row of seared cotton, and the precipitous piney woods ensnarled in the sleeping kudzu, and the

little secluded hamlets of the black prairies with their weak and trembling lights
and worn facades and bereft thoroughfares. Asphalt Thomas would be at the
wheel, and dead leaves swirled on the highway and insects splattered against
the windows in the departing counterfeit spring, and the older players in their
mad and boisterous horseplay, which by his bemused demeanor the coach
himself seemed vaguely to elicit after a victory:

"Hey, Coach, can't we go no *faster*?"

From behind the steering wheel, looking straight ahead: "You don't deserve to
go no faster. We only beat them fairies ten points."

"Hey, Coach, let's stop for some *beer*!"

"The way *you* played, you'd vomit up Pet milk."

Their names were Clarence, Thomas, Jerry, Calvin, John Ed, Percy, Verner
Ray, their nicknames being "Bouncer," "Noggin," "Steak Lips" (for reasons ob-
vious to all), "Termite" (shortened to the more manageable "Term"), "White
Boy" (his full name being Clarence White), "Muttonhead" (because his head was
shaped like a sheep), and "Blue" (because he was Syrian, and the others claimed
he *looked* blue). Who would forget the crackerbox gymnasia of these poor little
towns—the old hissing radiators, the narrow erstwhile locker rooms crawling
with water bugs and roaches, the pony-tailed cheerleaders in saddle oxfords and
pleated mid-calf skirts, the white wooden backboards and cheap tacky panelling,
the abandoned elevated stages where a few dozen spectators sat on portable
green bleachers—the benches and scorers' table right up to the out-of-bounds
lines, the ancient round clocks with the swooping second hands, better than the
digital ones later, tying you more truly to *time* because not so stark and precise—
a little like life itself in its passing? When Term or Blue churlishly complained of
the conditions, Asphalt would rejoin: "Fancier than what *I* played on at your age.
You're spoiled as a shithouse rat." The walls stood so close to the floor that White
Boy made a basket while running fast and sprinted right through a door into an
empty classroom and knocked over several chairs and desks.

If Asphalt Thomas vilified *us* during practices, imagine his conduct with the
referees. "They don't know whether I'm gonna kiss 'em on the mouth or kick
their ass," he would say of his own shifting cajoleries and rages, his sly supplica-
tions and venomous ill tempers. Once during a time out he accosted one of them
and whispered: "Ain't it about time you get your damned *cataracts* took out, Ran-
dy?" and withdrew his big grey pocketknife, and on another tense occasion said
to a hairless and vociferous Italian among their number, "You screamin' dago!
You're bald as a gorilla's nuts," which earned him not one but *two* technical fouls,

Asphalt later philosophically explaining: "That's because a gorilla's got two nuts, like everybody else." The partisans in these tough little towns, adults and students in equal fervor, cursed and defiled our team, considering us metropolitans, and an angry echelon in one of them threw rocks and empty bottles at us as we rushed from the gymnasium to the bus, and Asphalt Thomas herded us aboard and then stood briefly at the driver's door and shook his fist at them and shouted: "You scraggly-ass pointy-head peckerwoods! You don't know basketball from cuckoo squat!" but even he would wisely drive us out of there in a hurry.

My girlfriend Georgia merely tolerated the sport of basketball. She would go to the home games, usually sitting alone, or sometimes with Mrs. Idella King, the English teacher, who was scarcely aware of the rules and regulations but attended out of fealty to her unlikely protégé, Asphalt Thomas. The team roster was now depleted to eight, and one day after practice Asphalt Thomas pulled me aside. "I gotta use you a little tomorrow night. Don't drink no milk or Cokes or water. Don't drink nuthin'. Get a good night's rest. Pray to the Lord. My boys are droppin' like flies." I tossed and turned in my sleep, and all the next day my stomach churned with a million wavy butterflies. Sure enough, with four minutes to go and a nine-point lead Asphalt Thomas looked down my way. "Get in there for Blue. He looks like he's ready to throw up." I felt naked as I entered my first varsity game, and glacial and cold in my joints. It turned out all right. "You just lost your cherry," the coach said to me afterwards. "Didn't do much harm at all." In the next game three nights later I played a few minutes and was as self-satisfied as I had ever been in making six points against the lumbering and unfortunate team from Tuckaho. An *athlete*? Hardly yet. Moody and distracted as ever, my mother was frantic on the subject. "It's *dangerous*," she said. "You're going to get hurt, I know it. They're better than you. Wait and see. *You're going to get hurt!*"

That year was Fisk's Landing's turn to have the conference high school basketball tournament. These were flatland boroughs more or less the size of our own, summoned from the anxiety and ambiguity of the flatland of those times to our place (a funny league, to tell the truth, and not especially good in basketball, stepchild as this was to the football gridiron, but who would volunteer to admit it?) and the town had sought to embellish itself for its incipient visitors. Why did little American towns come so alive then for outsiders? Was it from fear of seeming paltry before their own eyes? Of assuaging their own day-to-day isolation? Or in this instance had death's specter itself, the returning Korean dead, spurred the urge of release? There were directional posters on the lightposts—self-flattery indeed to think someone might get lost here—historical signs in front of

the old houses, crimson-and-white bunting on the storefronts, and an enormous multi-colored streamer on the courthouse: "Welcome, King Cotton Conference!" The yellow out-of-town school buses were everywhere, and dozens of cars with the license plates bearing the alien county names, and in the afternoons the cheerleaders from the other towns strutted the narrow streets around the school. Asphalt Thomas was in his utmost element, and ubiquitous, offering directions to all comers, talking basketball in agitated little clusters with the rival coaches, one of whom had been his teammate on the land-grant university team, exchanging high-flown felicities with the visiting principals and superintendents—"I'm gonna be one of them *principals* when I hang up the jock," he said to me of them—"just as well get used to my future *colleagues*." The gymnasium was packed for the competition: Thursday and Friday matches, both boys and girls, then the semi-finals and finals all Saturday, and the festive containment of organized celebration reminded one a little of Fisk's Landing Christmas.

Early in our first game, Blue sprained his ankle and had to leave for the season. Then, toward the end of the third quarter it finally happened, as I knew with dire inevitability that it would and must—White Boy crashed mightily to the floor near our bench with two adversaries asprawl him, and his wail of distress rose up and filled the noisome and crowded assembly, suddenly mute now as he grimaced in honest pain, heaving and sputtering on the hardwood like a fallen sparrow, his whole left arm protruding outward from his torso at a grotesque, unholy angle.

Asphalt Thomas chewed his gum as he bent before the stricken warrior. "Can you fix him?" he asked the manager-trainer Leon, who was examining the injury.

"Nossir, Coach. This thing's broke."

"Hurts like shit," Blue said. "Gimme a shot, Leon."

"I'm jinxed," the coach said after he comforted the contorted victim as he was led away to the hospital. "What the devil did I do to deserve this?" Then he dubiously turned to me. "Well. . . ."

This was the big time. I was consumed with the same dry-mouthed giddiness the first day I kissed Georgia. Please, I silently beseeched the entire Anglican hierarchy: No mistakes. The prayer was in its fashion answered. Playing the entire final quarter I committed no blunders, but for that matter did not make a single contribution that to this day I can recall—an invisible entity, more or less, if ever there was one. Luckily our squad was leading by several points when the quarter began. The opponents were big and aggressive but slow and cumbersome, and we won.

But the next morning, Friday, when my dog Dusty woke me with a copious lick or two to the nose as usual, my whole lower right foot was a terrible blood blister. From my toes down to the arch was a pool of blood, covered with bursting membrane. I had had two or three before, but nothing ever like this one. I have an almost Quaker distaste of blood, so one can imagine the horror with which I greeted this sight; to my surprise, however, I did not faint, or even retch. I must have hurt it the night before, somewhere late in the game, but I had thought it only a bruise. Now, on this morning as I got out of bed, I could barely walk, the massive blister mocking one's efforts, indeed as I see now perhaps even one's very youth itself. I stripped off my pajamas and looked myself over. From a blow I remembered to the thigh, I perceived I even had a charley horse. Asphalt Thomas once told the team charley horses were inevitable for ball players, as if ordained by the Old Testament, and he also often surmised that blood blisters were the price one paid for being fast and a little bow-legged, as I was and am—not fast now, but still a little bow-legged. Nonetheless it was humiliating to discover one had *both*, and this after a scant and obscure and lusterless quarter.

I knew I had to get out of the house quickly, before my mother found me in harm's way, for her reaction would have been little shy of epileptic in its magnitude. Happily she and her dance students were leaving that afternoon for a two-day recital in the capital city and would not return until Sunday. Now I put my ear to the door, and was for the first time grateful for the sounds of the tap dancing in front. I was tempted to telephone Georgia to come get me in her car, but decided to make my own way. Ordering Dusty to stay, I limped out the back porch and detoured through Mrs. Griffin's yard to the boulevard, hitchhiking a ride with a schoolmate's father to the schoolhouse. I hobbled toward Mrs. Idella King's homeroom. Great stabs of pain were shooting around my foot, and then the charley horse started to throb too; my whole lower body was insufferable, and this made me feel both angry and vulnerable, especially angry. I had never really been hurt before, and this was a new moment in life. My thoughts went out to the official military escorts accompanying the hometown dead from Korea who had converged on Fisk's Landing with missing ears, fingers, and toes.

Georgia was tarrying inside the main entrance under the Plato statue just before the bell. "I waited for you. Are you hurt?"

In time's perspective I probably should have been proud of my wounds in front of Georgia, an honorable gladiator representing his school no matter how ineffectually, as in the Baptist preachers' oft-mentioned tale of the poor crippled lad who ran in the race because he was all his town had. But the thought of the pool of blood in the blister left no room for heroic pretensions.

"Good game," Mrs. King said. After roll call she took me to the back of the classroom and got me to take off my shoe and sock. Georgia and three or four others came over to watch. The sight of Mrs. King bending down in her black dress with the Phi Beta Kappa key dangling from her necklace to examine one's own blood blister was unflattering, and the way the other students stared down at me as if I were little more than an experimental cadaver in a windowless morgue was discomfiting. "Asphalt should see this," Mrs. King said.

She wrote me out a hall pass. I went down the corridor to the coach's office under the gymnasium, but he was not there. "He's teachin' driver's ed first period," Leon told me as he tossed last night's uniforms into the washing machine. "You hurt, ain't you? You sure *look* hurt." I attended the first class, then went to the gym again. Asphalt Thomas was sitting in the little cubbyhole adjoining our locker room, a dip of snuff lodged in his nether lip. "Let's see." Again I removed the shoe and sock.

"*Whew!* Worst I ever saw," he said, spitting all the while into a paper cup and gazing philosophically at the foot. "We'll handle it. We don't play again til tomorrow anyhow. Besides, we're down to the bottom of the barrel." He reached in a drawer of a battered oak desk, rummaged around, and brought out a long needle. He also withdrew a box of Diamond matches and began to heat the end of the needle.

Do we have to do this? I remember asking.

"Turn your head, then," he said. "Prop up the foot."

I closed my eyes. There was a quick, sharp pain, accompanied by an audible *swoosh.* When I opened my eyes again, there were splashes of blood on the dingy walls.

"Have to wash that damned stuff off," he said. "Now *that* was a blood blister. Where's Leon? *Leon!*" Leon came in with a wet rag and cleaned up the mess.

"It's okay now," Asphalt said. "Don't even need wrappin'. I got twenty against Vandy on the road after a blood blister bad as that." The blister was indeed subsiding, like a derelict hose after the water had gone through, and it felt better already, the lifting of a weight. From a bottle Asphalt now applied a generous amount of tough-skin, the cure-all of the era. He used half a bottle, and the smell was piquant.

"Got a little charley, Leon said? How come you so beat up? You only played a *quarter.* Got to protect yourself better. Use the elbows when the zebras ain't

lookin'. And I don't mean chicken wings, I mean real *elbows*." Now he examined my thigh. Then he handed me a tube of analgesic, the hot kind—"Red Hot Kramer" on the tube itself, or known to us colloquially as "Atomic Balm." I rubbed most of it into the skin. "Just go ahead and empty the fucker," he suggested. "We got a year's supply." After that he and Leon wrapped the thigh in an Ace bandage, then put about five yards of adhesive around it. "Don't take this off til after the finals," he said, "if we get to the finals. You can take showers in it. It's waterproof. Just shake your leg and limber up every little while. Can't let it get stiff, like a dick. Maybe run some in the back this afternoon. Idella might let you out of class to run some. You're a rookie and damaged goods, but all I got. Got to play with pain. Pain never hurt a real player. The Lord's testin' you. Keep your brain off the foot and on the game. I always played best hurtin'. Sank twenty-four against Auburn with a busted-up nose with blood for snot."

His admonition rang hollow in my head when that afternoon during study hall I went out in a sweatsuit behind the gymnasium to loosen up my leg. It was cold and clear, not a cloud in a matchless azure sky, and a flock of wood ducks flew in pristine V-formation overhead. There was a girls' game in the gym, and the noises of the crowd drifted out that way. Four or five of the cheerleaders from Monroe City, planters' daughters, were resting on the lawn; I recognized them from the school dances in the flatland. "What's wrong with *you*?" one of them inquired. "You smell like a drug store." They drew back in mock sympathy, slouching as they had learned from their mothers in the plutocratic flatland manner, hips arched high, hands angular on each side of them. "How's that Georgia?" And they laughed inanely and chattered in the timeless flatland persiflage like a skittish cluster of parakeets as I circled the field again.

The omniscient Asphalt Thomas had observed this tableau from the back door of the locker room. I knew he had been there because of the sound of his jangling keys, his keys to every room and closet and alcove and recess in the entire school building. "Showin' off to the little gals," he said as I came in, "them silly little spoiled rich gals that giggle all the time. Better go home and soak the leg and don't drink the water and sleep twelve hours."

The team went into the semi-finals the next afternoon, Saturday, against Monroe City, people overflowing into the balcony and hallways, some propped on boxes and ladders and watching through the high windows outside, and there was a good flavor of bourbon everywhere.

Merely adequate as I was, playing most of the game and scoring a paltry four points, the remaining seniors, Muttonhead, Term, Noggin, Bouncer, performed with such deft and unexpected nobility that Asphalt Thomas called it the best-played game of the season. In the closing minutes one of the opposition's Notreangelo boys (they had three) whacked me across the back of my neck with his clenched fist when the referees were somewhere else. *"Kick the bastard out!"* I heard the shout from the grandstand. It was unmistakably Georgia, and I learned later that several of the surrounding onlookers stared at her coldly for long moments, and a pastor's wife complained to Idella King, who replied in words that ring down to me now: "Well, they *should* have kicked him out." Fisk's Landing prevailed by six points and would play in that night's championship.

Dizzied, throbbing, I soaked myself under the water spout of the shower. My thigh under the elastic bandage was burning hot, my foot an enormous palpitation. I asked Asphalt Thomas for a bandage on the foot. Once more he looked it over. It was crimson at the bottom now, with shrivelled skin at the edges, but yellow too from the plentitude of medicine. It looked awful. "Naw," he said. "The blood has to circulate. It's healin' real nice." Leon gave me three aspirin, then applied more tough-skin, so that I looked like a leper there.

Having defeated Monroe City and the Notreangelos, we would play the last match for the trophy, which Fisk's Landing had not won in ten years, at nine that evening, four hours away. Our adversary would be the only accomplished team in the conference, Lutherville, with the best and most adept player in that league, the all-state Number 8, averaging twenty points a game. Our game would follow the girls' finals.

All high school locker rooms have likely smelled the same since time began. The mingling scents of ammonia, analgesic, tough-skin, iodine, and the Chlorox bleach of Leon doing the washing as we waited for Asphalt Thomas on that distant afternoon linger with me now, so that the assembled odor of it is still as real to me as any I have ever known.

When everyone was ready Asphalt Thomas got us together there for a talk. Unlike at school, he dressed up for the games, as if paying a kind of pious sartorial obeisance to the sport itself, and on this day he wore a sleeveless half-buttoned wool sweater over a shirt and tie, the tie so short that it did not even reach to his midriff. "You men sucked it up out there today. I'm proud of you. See what you can do when your mind's off the snatch?" He told us to go home and relax and not eat too much. "Don't even *think* about losin', for Chrissake.

Tell your mommas to cook you a small hamburger steak or somethin' like that, but no *grease*." He wanted us back an hour and a half before the game, he added, because he was working on a special defense against Lutherville. "We once tried this against LSU," he said, "when they had a big ol' center and damned tricky guard. We got to hold down Number 8 and Number 20. But don't worry your heads til you get back. Then we'll worry. Let's whip their maggot-ridden asses. What are we—men or mice?" As the others filed out, he took me aside. "You're on Number 8. I ain't got no choice." Number 8!

Georgia drove me around town for a while. Fisk's Landing was striking in this dying afternoon. The out-of-towners were milling about the courthouse and the main street, spilling in and out of the restaurants, cruising the boulevard in their cars admiring the houses. The green-and-white crepe of Lutherville abounded, and near the Elk's Club the impromptu cheers of their assembled students filled the brisk twilight. On the next corner I even sighted the Notreangelo who had whacked me in the neck only two hours before. He was standing there with his tough upper-flatland chums, including his snarling, swarthy siblings, and when he saw me he stared in haughty and immured disdain.

We went to Georgia's parents, who had promised something to eat. Then she and I sat on the front porch. The air felt good. It was getting on to dark now and the blow on the neck was beginning to hurt for the first time since the game; little shooting stars would appear before my eyes when I turned my head, and the blistered foot was all but numb. I wondered why I had ever voluntarily gotten into this, for in that moment it really did not make good sense. Was there an Anglican prayer against Number 8?

"I've thought of you all day. You look funny." Kneeling before me she took off my shoe—everyone seemed to want to take off my shoe—and gently massaged my foot.

From the school across the street the crowds were congregating for the girls' game. Georgia's mother and father came out the door on the way to the gym. At Georgia's caressing touch I had felt a surprising swell at my thighs, and I hid them quickly with my hands. "Kick a little tail, boy," her father said. Her mother tentatively assessed us as Georgia rubbed the foot. "Are you going to the midnight show after the game?" she asked. "Yes'm," Georgia said, and we all departed toward the school.

In the locker room toward the end of the girls' game, Asphalt Thomas had the big portable blackboard with his X's and O's, and he went over them meticulously—a floating zone around the basket against the tall Number 20,

man-to-man on Number 8. Then he just stood there for a second summoning his words. He often dropped scriptural references into his terse pre-game speeches, sometimes claiming a large regard for religion, although I suspected he did not believe any of it to be true—had he lost it on Okinawa? "Get out there and *fight*, men! Run out on that friggin' court with your hand in the hand of the greatest coach of all times—not me, but the head coach from Nazareth." Just before we went out he approached me again. His eyes were glistening as he sat on his haunches and whispered, "If Number 8 bends down to tie his damned shoelace, you bend down and untie it. If he goes to the commode to take a crap, you follow him and lock him in. If he spits, you spit." I sat there before him on the locker room bench. "You scared? Nervous? When I was eighteen years old," he said, "I crawled halfway across every damn island the Pacific had, on my belly, scared shitless. Think about that when you get out there." We put tough-skin on our hands before leaving. As the home team, Asphalt said, we would start off with a fairly old ball. If the zebras brought in a new, slick ball, we had more tough-skin on the bench. In the warm-ups, the tough-skin with the old balls made the shooting easy, as all basketball boys of that time with tough-skin on their hands and old balls to shoot know and remember.

Number 8 was the swiftest I had seen, and smart, and also a gentleman. His fakes left you breathless. "Keep away, keep away!" he would shout nervously as he moved, but he would never have whacked one across the neck with the referees not watching as the Monroe City Notreangelo had done. He was only an inch or so taller than I, but heavier, and two years older, and I was no match for him; nothing I had ever learned had prepared me for this public humiliation. Why had Asphalt Thomas allowed me to play the entire game? Our team was beaten badly.

Right at the final buzzer I ran into the wall after a loose ball and was sitting against it on the floor. The game was done, and the Lutherville people were rushing onto the court to cut down the nets, their cheerleaders performing one somersault after another on the hardwood. Blood was oozing a little from my shoe and my mouth felt full of cotton. Number 8 came over and sat down next to me. "Damn, I'm tired," he said, and extended his hand. Three years later he would be all-Southeastern Conference at the state university, and honorable mention all-America. And here, too, is the yellowed clipping from the *Sentinel* in front of me now:

Kent "Lightnin" Boult, all-state standout of Lutherville, scored 28 points Saturday night and wrecked Fisk's Landing's defenses as the Bobcats defeated the valiant but injury-riddled Choctaws, 56–33, for the conference crown.

As a man Asphalt Thomas was streaked with raw violence, yet he had a curious begrudging tenderness in him which always surprised me at age sixteen, the ferocity and the care existing there in odd and unexpected tandem. In the locker room after the game he cuffed me gently on the head. "Don't worry, kid," he said. "You're young. You *learned.* Put on some weight. Use the elbows more. Work on the jumper."

Almost everyone was gone. I was the last to leave, except of course for Leon. Georgia was waiting under a young oak on the campus. In the pungent shadows was the promise of early spring. Across the street from where we met were the two Negro shacks, hushed now except for the woman on the front stoop of one of them tending to a bawling infant.

"Are you all right?"

I was okay.

"You played good."

"Oh, come on."

"Well, you did. *I* think you did."

For years, I had an ugly burn on my thigh from the analgesic under the bandage. There is still to this day, as I age, a slight remnant of the burn there, and sometimes I look at it and remember those days. But mostly, really, as the years pass, I do not think much about losing to Lutherville, or the ingenious Number 8, before the packed house at home. I merely recall how I was hurting after that game, and Georgia there, and in the parked sedan how gentle she was with my wounds, her tender touch, and the mingling pleasure and pain.

Baseball

The Phantom of Yazoo

MEMOIR

Mark Twain and his comrades growing up a century before in another village on the other side of the Mississippi, my friends and I had but one sustaining ambition in the 1940s. Theirs in Hannibal was to be steamboatmen, ours in Yazoo was to be major-league baseball players. In the summers, we thought and talked of little else. We memorized batting averages, fielding averages, slugging averages, we knew the roster of the Cardinals and the Red Sox better than their own managers must have known them, and to hear the broadcasts from all the big-city ballparks with their memorable names—the Polo Grounds, Wrigley Field, Fenway Park, the Yankee Stadium—was to set our imagination churning for the glory and riches those faraway places would one day bring us. One of our friends went to St. Louis on his vacation to see the Cards, and when he returned with the autographs of Stan Musial, Red Schoendienst, Country Slaughter, Marty Marion, Joe Garagiola, and a dozen others, we could hardly keep down our envy. I hated that boy for a month, and secretly wished him dead, not only because he took on new airs but because I wanted those scraps of paper with their magic characters. I wished also that my own family were wealthy enough to take me to a big-league town for two weeks, but to a bigger place even than St. Louis: Chicago, maybe, with not one but two teams, or best of all to New York, with three. I had bought a baseball cap in Jackson, a real one from the Brooklyn Dodgers, and a Jackie Robinson Louisville Slugger, and one day when I could not even locate any of the others for catch or for baseball talk, I sat on a curb on Grand Avenue with the most dreadful feelings of being caught forever by time—trapped there always in my scrawny and helpless condition. *I'm ready, I'm ready*, I kept thinking to myself, but that remote future when I would wear a cap like that and be a hero for a grandstand full of people seemed so far away I knew it would never come. I must have been the most dejected-looking child you ever saw, sitting hunched up on the curb and dreaming of glory in the mythical cities of the North. I felt worse when a carload of high school boys halted right in front of where I sat, and they started reciting what they always did when they saw me alone and day-dreaming: *Wee Willie Winkie walks through the town, upstairs and downstairs in his nightgown.* Then one of them said, "Winkie, you *gettin'* much?" "You bastards!" I shouted, and they drove off laughing like wild men.

Almost every afternoon when the heat was not unbearable my father and I would go out to the old baseball field behind the armory to hit flies. I would stand far out in center field, and he would station himself with a fungo at home plate, hitting me one high fly, or Texas Leaguer, or line drive after another, sometimes for an hour or more without stopping. My dog would get out there in the outfield with me, and retrieve the inconsequential dribblers or the ones that went too far. I was light and speedy, and could make the most fantastic catches, turning completely around and forgetting the ball sometimes to head for the spot where it would descend, or tumbling head-on for a diving catch. The smell of that new-cut grass was the finest of all smells, and I could run forever and never get tired. It was a dreamy, suspended state, those late afternoons, thinking of nothing but outfield flies, as the world drifted lazily by on Jackson Avenue. I learned to judge what a ball would do by instinct, heading the way it went as if I owned it, and I knew in my heart I could make the big time. Then, after all that exertion, my father would shout, "I'm whupped!" and we would quit for the day.

When I was twelve I became a part-time sportswriter for the *Yazoo Herald*, whose courtly proprietors allowed me unusual independence. I wrote up an occasional high school or Legion game in a florid prose, filled with phrases like "two-ply blow" and "circuit-ringer." My mentor was the sports editor of the Memphis *Commercial Appeal*, whose name was Walter Stewart, a man who could invest the most humdrum athletic contest with the elements of Shake-spearean tragedy. I learned whole paragraphs of his by heart, and used some of his expressions for my reports on games between Yazoo and Satartia, or the other teams. That summer when I was twelve, having never seen a baseball game higher than the Jackson Senators of Class B, my father finally relented and took me to Memphis to see the Chicks, who were Double-A. It was the farthest I had ever been from home, and the largest city I had ever seen; I walked around in a state of joyousness, admiring the crowds and the big park high above the river, and best of all, the grand old lobby of the Chisca Hotel.

Staying with us at the Chisca were the Nashville Vols, who were there for a big series with the Chicks. I stayed close to the lobby to get a glimpse of them; when I discovered they spent all day, up until the very moment they left for the ball-park, playing the pinball machine, I stationed myself there too. Their names were Tookie Gilbert, Smokey Burgess, Chuck Workman, and Bobo Hollomon, the latter being the one who got as far as the St. Louis Browns, pitched a no-hitter in his first major-league game, and failed to win another before being shipped down forever to obscurity; one afternoon my father and I ran into them outside the hotel on the way to the game and gave them a ride in our taxi. I could have been fit for tying, especially when Smokey Burgess tousled my hair and asked me if I batted right or left, but when I listened to them as they grumbled about having to get out to the ballpark so early, and complained about the season having two more damned months to go and about how ramshackle their team bus was, I was too disillusioned even to tell my friends when I got home.

Because back home, even among the adults, baseball was all-meaning; it was the link with the outside. A place known around town simply as The Store, down near the train depot, was the principal center of this ferment. The Store had sawdust on the floor and long shreds of flypaper hanging from the ceiling. Its most familiar staples were Rexall supplies, oysters on the half shell, legal beer, and illegal whiskey, the latter served up, Mississippi bootlegger style, by the bottle from a hidden shelf and costing not merely the price of the whiskey but the investment in gas required to go to Louisiana to fetch it. There was a long count-er in the back. On one side of it, the white workingmen congregated after hours every afternoon to compare the day's scores and talk batting averages, and on the other side, also talking baseball, were the Negroes, juxtaposed in a face-to-face arrangement with the whites. The scores were chalked up on a blackboard hanging on a red-and-purple wall, and the conversations were carried on in fast, galloping shouts from one end of the room to the other. An intelligent white boy of twelve was even permitted, in that atmosphere of heady freedom before anyone knew the name of Justice Warren or had heard much of the United States Supreme Court, a quasi-public position favoring the Dodgers, who had Jackie Robinson, Roy Campanella, and Don Newcombe—not to mention, so it was rumored, God knows how many Chinese and mulattoes being groomed in the minor leagues. I remember my father turned to some friends at The Store one day and observed, "Well, you can say what you want to about that nigger Robinson, but he's got *guts*," and to a man the others nodded, a little reluctantly, but in agreement nonetheless. And one of them said he had read somewhere that Pee Wee Reese, a white southern boy, was the best friend Robinson had on the team, which proved they had chosen the right one to watch after him.

There were two firehouses in town, and on hot afternoons the firemen at both establishments sat outdoors in their shirtsleeves, with the baseball broadcast turned up as loud as it would go. On his day off work my father, who had left Cities Service and was now a bookkeeper for the wholesale grocery, usually started with Firehouse No. 1 for the first few innings and then hit No. 2 before ending up at The Store for the post-game conversations.

I decided not to try out for the American Legion Junior Baseball team that summer. Legion baseball was an important thing for country boys in those parts, but I was too young and skinny, and I had heard that the coach, a dirt farmer known as Gentleman Joe, made his protégés lie flat in the infield while he walked on their stomachs; he also forced them to take three-mile runs through the streets of town, talked them into going to church, and persuaded them to give up Coca-Colas. A couple of summers later, when I did go out for the team, I found out that Gentleman Joe did in fact insist on these soul-strengthening rituals; because of them, we won the Mississippi state championship and the merchants in town took up a collection and sent us all the way to St. Louis to see the Cards play the Phillies. My main concern that earlier summer, however, lay in the more academic aspects of the game. I knew more about baseball, its technology and its ethos, than all the firemen and Store experts put together. Having read most of its literature, I could give a sizable lecture on the infield-fly rule alone, which only a thin minority of the townspeople knew existed. Gentleman Joe was held in some esteem for his strategical sense, yet he was the only man I ever knew who could call for a sacrifice bunt with two men out and not have a bad conscience about it. I remember one dismaying moment that occurred while I was watching a country semi-pro game. The home team had runners on first and third with one

out, when the batter hit a ground ball to the first baseman, who stepped on first and then threw to second. The shortstop, covering second, stepped on the base but made no attempt to tag the runner. The man on third had crossed the plate, of course, but the umpire, who was not very familiar with the subtleties of the rules, signaled a double play. Sitting in the grandstand, I knew that it was not a double play at all and that the run had scored, but when I went down, out of my Christian duty, to tell the manager of the local team that he had just been done out of a run, he told me I was crazy. This was the kind of brainpower I was up against.

That summer the local radio station, the one where we broadcast our Methodist programs, started a baseball quiz program. A razor blade company offered free blades and the station chipped in a dollar, all of which went to the first listener to telephone with the·right answer to the day's baseball question. If there was no winner, the next day's pot would go up a dollar. At the end of the month they had to close down the program because I was winning all the money. It got so easy, in fact, that I stopped phoning in the answers some afternoons so that the pot could build up and make my winnings more spectacular. I netted about twenty-five dollars and a ten-year supply of double-edged, smooth-contact razor blades before they gave up. One day, when the jackpot was a mere two dollars, the announcer tried to confuse me. "Babe Ruth," he said, "hit sixty home runs in 1927 to set the major-league record. What man had the next-highest total?" I telephoned and said, "George Herman Ruth. He hit fifty-nine in another season." My adversary, who had developed an acute dislike of me, said that was not the correct answer. He said it should have been *Babe* Ruth. This incident angered me, and I won for the next four days, just for the hell of it.

On Sunday afternoons we sometimes drove out of town and along hot, dusty roads to baseball fields that were little more than parched red clearings, the outfield sloping out of the woods and ending in some tortuous gully full of yellowed paper, old socks, and vintage cow shit. One of the backwoods teams had a fastball pitcher named Eckert, who didn't have any teeth, and a fifty-year-old left-handed catcher named Smith. Since there were no catcher's mitts made for left-handers, Smith had to wear a mitt on his throwing hand. In his simian posture he would catch the ball and toss it lightly into the air and then whip his mitt off and catch the ball in his bare left hand before throwing it back. It was a wonderfully lazy way to spend those Sunday afternoons—my father and my friends and I sitting in the grass behind the chicken-wire backstop with eight or ten dozen farmers, watching the wrong-handed catcher go through his contorted gyrations, and listening at the same time to our portable radio, which brought us the rising inflections of a baseball announcer called the Old Scotchman. The sounds of the two games, our own and the one being broadcast from Brooklyn or Chicago, merged and rolled across the bumpy outfield and the gully into the woods; it was a combination that seemed perfectly natural to everyone there.

I can see the town now on some hot, still weekday afternoon in mid-summer: ten thousand souls and nothing doing. Even the red water truck was a diversion, coming slowly up Grand Avenue with its sprinklers on full force, the water making sizzling steam-clouds on the pavement while half-naked Negro children followed the truck up the street and played in the torrent until they got soaking wet. Over on Broadway, where the old men sat drowsily in straw chairs on the pavement near the Bon-Ton Café, whittling to make the time pass, you could laze around on the sidewalks—barefoot, if your feet were tough enough to stand the scalding concrete—watching the big cars with out-of-state plates whip by, the driver hardly knowing and certainly not caring what place this was. Way up that fantastic hill, Broadway seemed to end in a seething mist—little heat mirages that shimmered off the asphalt; on the main street itself there would be only a handful of cars parked here and there, and the merchants and the lawyers sat in the shade under their broad awnings, talking slowly, aimlessly, in the cryptic summer way. The one o'clock whistle at the sawmill would send out its loud bellow, reverberating up the streets to the bend in the Yazoo River, hardly making a ripple in the heavy somnolence.

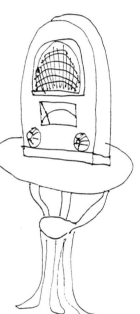

But by two o'clock almost every radio in town was tuned in to the Old Scotchman. His rhetoric dominated the place. It hovered in the branches of the trees, bounced off the hills, and came out of the darkened stores; the merchants and the old men cocked their ears to him, and even from the big cars that sped by, their tires making lapping sounds in the softened highway, you could hear his voice, being carried past you out into the Delta.

The Old Scotchman's real name was Gordon McLendon, and he described the big-league games for the Liberty Broadcasting System, which had outlets mainly in the South and the Southwest. He had a deep, rich voice, and I think he was the best rhetorician, outside of Bilbo and Nye Bevan, I have ever heard. Under his handling a baseball game took on a life of its own. As in the prose of the *Commercial Appeal*'s Walter Stewart, his games were rare and remarkable entities; casual pop flies had the flow of history behind them, double plays resembled the stark clashes of old armies, and home runs deserved acknowledgment on earthen urns. Later, when I came across Thomas Wolfe, I felt I had heard him before, from Shibe Park, Crosley Field, or the Yankee Stadium.

One afternoon I was sitting around my house listening to the Old Scotchman, admiring the vivacity of a man who said he was a contemporary of Connie Mack. (I learned later that he was twenty-nine.) That day he was doing the Dodgers and the Giants from the Polo Grounds. The game, as I recall, was in the fourth inning, and the Giants were ahead by about 4 to 1. It was a boring game, however, and I began experimenting with my father's shortwave radio, an impressive mechanism a couple of feet wide, which had an aerial that almost touched the ceiling and the name of every major city in the world on its dial. It was by far the best radio I had ever seen; there was not another one like it in town. I switched the dial to shortwave and began picking up African drum music, French jazz, Australian weather reports, and a lecture from the British Broadcasting Company on the people who wrote poems for Queen Elizabeth. Then a curious thing happened. I came across a baseball game—the Giants and the Dodgers, from the Polo Grounds. After a couple of minutes I discovered that the game was in the eighth inning. I turned back to the local station, but here the Giants and Dodgers were still in the fourth. I turned again to the shortwave broadcast and listened to the last inning, a humdrum affair that ended with Carl Furillo popping out to shortstop, Gil Hodges grounding out second to first, and Roy Campanella lining out to center. Then I went back to the Old Scotchman and listened to the rest of the game. In the top of the ninth, an hour or so later, a ghostly thing occurred; to my astonishment and titillation, the game ended with Furillo popping out to short, Hodges grounding out second to first, and Campanella lining out to center.

I kept this unusual discovery to myself, and the next day, an hour before the Old Scotchman began his play-by-play of the second game of the series, I dialed the shortwave frequency, and, sure enough, they were doing the Giants and the Dodgers again. I learned that I was listening to the Armed Forces Radio Service, which broadcast games played in New York. As the game progressed I began jotting down notes on the action. When the first four innings were over I turned to the local station just in time to get the Old Scotchman for the first batter. The Old Scotchman's account of the game matched the shortwave's almost perfectly. The Scotchman's, in fact, struck me as being considerably more poetic than the one I had heard first. But I did not doubt him, since I could hear the roar of the crowd, the crack of the bat, and the Scotchman's precise description of foul balls that fell into the crowd, the gestures of the base coaches, and the expression on the face of a small boy who was eating a lemon popsicle in a box seat behind first base. I decided that the broadcast was being delayed somewhere along the line, maybe because we were so far from New York.

That was my first thought, but after a close comparison of the two broadcasts for the rest of the game, I sensed that something more sinister was taking place. For one thing, the Old Scotchman's description of the count on a batter, though it jibed 90 percent of the time, did not always match. For another, the Scotchman's crowd, compared with the other, kept up an ungodly noise. When Robinson stole second on shortwave, he did it without drawing a throw and without sliding, while for Mississippians the feat was performed in a cloud of angry, petulant dust. A foul ball that went over the grandstand and out of the park for shortwave listeners in Alaska, France, and the Argentine produced for the firemen, bootleggers, farmers, and myself a primitive scramble that ended with a feeble old lady catching the ball on the first bounce to the roar of an assembly that would have outnumbered Grant's at Old Cold Harbor. But the most revealing development came after the Scotchman's game was over. After the usual summaries, he mentioned that the game had been "recreated." I had never taken notice of that particular word before, because I lost interest once a game was over. I went to the dictionary, and under "recreate" I found, "To invest with fresh vigor and strength; to refresh, invigorate (nature, strength, a person or thing)." The Old Scotchman most assuredly invested a game with fresh vigor and strength, but this told me nothing. My deepest suspicions were confirmed, however, when I found the second definition of the word—"To create anew."

So there it was. I was happy to have fathomed the mystery, as perhaps no one else in the whole town had done. The Old Scotchman, for all his wondrous expressions, was not only several innings behind every game he described but was no doubt sitting in some air-conditioned studio in the hinterland, where he got the happenings of the game by news ticker; sound effects accounted for the crack of the bat and the crowd noises. Instead of being disappointed in the Scotchman, I was all the more pleased by his genius, for he made pristine facts more actual than actuality, a valuable lesson when the day finally came that I started reading literature. I must add, however, that this appreciation did not obscure the realization that I had at my disposal a weapon of unimaginable dimensions.

Next day I was at the shortwave again, but I learned with much disappointment that the game being broadcast on shortwave was not the one the Scotchman had chosen to describe. I tried every afternoon after that and discovered that I would have to wait until the Old Scotchman decided to do a game out of New York before I could match his game with the one described live on shortwave. Sometimes, I learned later, these coincidences did not occur for days; during an important Dodger or Yankee series, however, his game and that of the Armed Forces Radio Service often coincided for two or three days running. I was happy, therefore, to find, on an afternoon a few days later, that both the shortwave and the Scotchman were carrying the Yankees and the Indians.

I settled myself at the shortwave with notebook and pencil and took down every pitch. This I did for four full innings, and then I turned back to the town station, where the Old Scotchman was just beginning the first inning. I checked the first batter to make sure the accounts jibed. Then, armed with my notebook, I ran down the street to the corner grocery, a minor outpost of baseball intellection, presided over by my young Negro friend Bozo, a knowledgeable student of the game, the same one who kept my dog in bologna. I found Bozo behind the meat counter, with the Scotchman's account going full blast. I arrived at the interim between the top and bottom of the first inning.

"Who's pitchin' for the Yankees, Bozo?" I asked.

"They're pitchin' Allie Reynolds," Bozo said. "Old Scotchman says Reynolds really got the stuff today. He just set 'em down one, two, three."

The Scotchman, meanwhile, was describing the way the pennants were flapping in the breeze. Phil Rizzuto, he reported, was stepping to the plate.

"Bo," I said, trying to sound cut-and-dried, "you know what I think? I think Rizzuto's gonna take a couple of fast called strikes, then foul one down the left-field line, and then line out straight to Boudreau at short."

"Yeah?" Bozo said. He scratched his head and leaned lazily across the counter.

I went up front to buy something and then came back. The count worked to nothing and two on Rizzuto—a couple of fast called strikes and a foul down the left side. "This one," I said to Bozo, "he lines straight to Boudreau at short."

The Old Scotchman, pausing dramatically between words as was his custom, said, "Here's the windup on nothing and two. Here's the pitch on its way— there's a hard line drive! But Lou Boudreau's there at shortstop and he's got it. Phil hit that one on the nose, but Boudreau was right there."

Bozo looked over at me, his eyes bigger than they were. "How'd you know that?" he asked.

Ignoring this query, I made my second prediction. "Bozo," I said, "Tommy

Henrich's gonna hit the first pitch up against the right-field wall and slide in with a double."

"How come you think so?"

"Because I can predict anything that's gonna happen in baseball in the next ten years," I said. "I can tell you anything."

The Old Scotchman was describing Henrich at the plate. "Here comes the first pitch. Henrich swings, there's a hard smash into right field! . . . This one may be out of here! It's going, going—*no*! It's off the wall in right center, Henrich's rounding first, on his way to second. Here's the relay from Doby . . . Henrich slides in safely with a double!" The Yankee crowd sent up an awesome roar in the background.

"Say, how'd you know that?" Bozo asked. "How'd you know he was gonna wind up at second?"

"I just can tell. I got extra-vision," I said. On the radio, far in the background, the public-address system announced Yogi Berra. "Like Berra right now. You know what? He's gonna hit a one-one pitch down the right-field line—"

"How come you know?" Bozo said. He was getting mad.

"Just a second," I said. "I'm gettin' static." I stood dead still, put my hands up against my temples and opened my eyes wide. "Now it's comin' through clear. Yeah, Yogi's gonna hit a one-one pitch down the right-field line, and it's gonna be fair by about three or four feet—I can't say exactly—and Henrich's gonna score from second, but the throw is gonna get Yogi at second by a mile."

This time Bozo was silent, listening to the Scotchman, who described the ball and the strike, then said: "Henrich takes the lead off second. Benton looks over, stretches, delivers. Yogi swings." (There was the bat crack.) "There's a line drive down the right side! It's barely inside the foul line. It may go for extra bases! Henrich's rounding third and coming in with a run. Berra's moving toward second. Here comes the throw! . . . And they *get* him! They get Yogi easily on the slide at second!"

Before Bozo could say anything else, I reached in my pocket for my notes. "I've just written down here what I think's gonna happen in the first four innings," I said. "Like DiMag. See, he's gonna pop up to Mickey Vernon at first on a one-nothing pitch in just a minute. But don't you worry. He's gonna hit a 380-foot homer in the fourth with nobody on base on a full count. You just follow these notes and you'll see I can predict anything that's gonna happen in the next ten years." I handed him the paper, turned around, and left the store just as DiMaggio, on a one-nothing pitch, popped up to Vernon at first.

Then I went back home and took more notes from the shortwave. The Yanks clobbered the Indians in the late innings and won easily. On the local station, however, the Old Scotchman was in the top of the fifth inning. At this juncture I went to the telephone and called Firehouse No. 1.

"Hello," a voice answered. It was the fire chief.

"Hello, Chief, can you tell me the score?" I said. Calling the firehouse for baseball information was a common practice.

"The Yanks are ahead, 5–2."

"This is the Phantom you're talkin' with," I said.

"Who?"

"The Phantom. Listen carefully, Chief. Reynolds is gonna open this next inning with a pop-up to Doby. Then Rizzuto will single to left on a one-one count. Henrich's gonna force him at second on a two-and-one pitch but make it to first. Berra's gonna double to right on a nothing-and-one pitch, and Henrich's goin' to third. DiMaggio's gonna foul a couple off and then double down the left-field line, and both Henrich and Yogi are gonna score. Brown's gonna pop out to third to end the inning."

"Aw, go to hell," the chief said, and hung up.

This was precisely what happened, of course. I phoned No. 1 again after the inning.

"Hello."

"Hi. This is the Phantom again."

"Say, how'd you know that?"

"Stick with me," I said ominously, "and I'll feed you predictions. I can predict anything that's gonna happen anywhere in the next ten years." After a pause I added, "Beware of fire real soon," for good measure, and hung up.

I left my house and hurried back to the corner grocery. When I got there, the entire meat counter was surrounded by friends of Bozo's, about a dozen of them. They were gathered around my notes, talking passionately and shouting. Bozo saw me standing by the bread counter. "There he is! That's the one!" he declared. His colleagues turned and stared at me in undisguised awe. They parted respectfully as I strolled over to the meat counter and ordered a dime's worth of bologna for my dog.

A couple of questions were directed at me from the group, but I replied, "I'm sorry for what happened in the fourth. I predicted DiMag was gonna hit a full-count pitch for that homer. It came out he hit it on two-and-two. There was too much static in the air between here and New York."

"Too much *static?*" one of them asked.

"Yeah. Sometimes the static confuses my extra-vision. But I'll be back tomorrow if everything's okay, and I'll try not to make any more big mistakes."

"Big mistakes!" one of them shouted, and the crowd laughed admiringly, parting once more as I turned and left the store. I wouldn't have been at all surprised if they had tried to touch the hem of my shirt.

That day was only the beginning of my brief season of triumph. A schoolmate of mine offered me five dollars, for instance, to tell him how I had known that Johnny Mize was going to hit a two-run homer to break up one particularly close game for the Giants. One afternoon, on the basis of a lopsided first four innings, I had an older friend sneak into The Store and place a bet, which netted me $14.50. I felt so bad about it I tithed $1.45 in church the following Sunday. At Bozo's grocery store I was a full-scale oracle. To the firemen I remained the Phantom, and firefighting reached a peak of efficiency that month, simply because the firemen knew what was going to happen in the late innings and did not need to tarry when an alarm came.

One afternoon my father was at home listening to the Old Scotchman with a couple of out-of-town salesmen from Greenwood. They were sitting in the front room, and I had already managed to get the first three or four innings of the Cardinals and the Giants on paper before they arrived. The Old Scotchman was in the top of the first when I walked in and said hello. The men were talking business and listening to the game at the same time.

"I'm gonna make a prediction," I said. They stopped talking and looked at me. "I predict Musial's gonna take a ball and a strike and then hit a double to right field, scoring Schoendienst from second, but Marty Marion's gonna get tagged out at the plate."

"You're mighty smart," one of the men said. He suddenly sat up straight when the Old Scotchman reported, "Here's the windup and the pitch coming in. . . . Musial *swings!*" (Bat crack, crowd roar.) "He drives one into right field! This one's going up against the boards! . . . Schoendienst rounds third. He's coming on in to score! Marion dashes around third, legs churning. His cap falls off, but here he *comes*! Here's the toss to the plate. He's nabbed at home. He is *out* at the plate! Musial holds at second with a run-producing double."

Before I could parry the inevitable questions, my father caught me by the elbow and hustled me into a back room. "How'd you know that?" he asked.

"I was just guessin'," I said. "It was nothin' but luck."

He stopped for a moment, and then a new expression showed on his face. "Have *you* been callin' the firehouse?" he asked.

"Yeah, I guess a few times."

"Now, you tell me how you found out about all that. I mean it."

When I told him about the shortwave, I was afraid he might be mad, but on the contrary he laughed uproariously. "Do you remember these next few innings?" he asked.

"I got it all written down," I said, and reached in my pocket for the notes. He took the notes and told me to go away. From the yard, a few minutes later, I heard him predicting the next inning to the salesmen.

A couple of days later, I phoned No. 1 again. "This is the Phantom," I said. "With two out, Branca's gonna hit Stinky Stanky with a fast ball, and then Alvin Dark's gonna send him home with a triple."

"Yeah, we know it," the fireman said in a bored voice. "We're listenin' to a shortwave too. You think you're somethin', don't you? You're Ray Morris's boy."

I knew everything was up. The next day, as a sort of final gesture, I took some more notes to the corner grocery in the third or fourth inning. Some of the old crowd was there, but the atmosphere was grim. They looked at me coldly. "Oh, man," Bozo said, "*we* know the Old Scotchman ain't at that game. He's four or five innings behind. He's makin' all that stuff up." The others grumbled and turned away. I slipped quietly out the door.

My period as a seer was over, but I went on listening to the shortwave broadcasts out of New York a few days more. Then, a little to my surprise, I went back to the Old Scotchman, and in time I found that the firemen, the bootleggers, and the few dirt farmers who had shortwave sets all did the same. From then on, accurate, up-to-the-minute baseball news was in disrepute there. I believe we all went back to the Scotchman not merely out of loyalty but because, in our great isolation, he touched our need for a great and unmitigated eloquence.

Me and Ollie

F I C T I O N

 ome on,

I said. "Let's go hit some flies."

We passed on through the business section of downtown Yazoo, barren and sedate on this day, and went to the vacant lot where we always played. It was an old corn field grown over with grass. Because of its location between the black and white sections of town, it had become a meeting place where boys of different races could come and play ball.

They were greedy then, I see now as I age, the unmanly men who ran the town from their big houses, and their unmanly women: greedy to keep us away, Ollie and me and the others, way back then. Their greed was thought out and is to this God's day still greedy. Don't play ball with them, they said, you can't work them to death if you start playing ball. They were older and knew things a lot better. In their Biblical rapine they didn't want us to play ball, and they knew their own thinking, and they believed they were right. Yet their greed didn't comprehend the smell of the grass along the river and the smack of the bat, and in the languishing moments, the sweet, funny, scary heat of the ball up on the Yazoo spaces—before the ball descended and you went for it, always wanting the ball. They couldn't predict that.

My friends fanned out in the field with Skip, my dog, at their heels, and I started hitting fly balls to them, each in his own turn. With the first clean crack of bat against ball, I began to relax, forgetting for the moment about the rumors of witchcraft that were sweeping the vicinity. Baseball is better than any demonology and will probably last longer. There's nothing prettier than the long, casual arch of a baseball against an azure and driftless April sky. Henjie pounded his glove and made a snappy catch, losing his glasses as he did so.

"Hummm-boy!" Bubba yelled.

They threw the ball around spiritedly to each other like infielders celebrating an out. Then Bubba tossed it back to me.

As I hit flies for them, the Yazoo River gently twisting and turning in the background, reflecting the distant sun in little prismatic sparkles, I lazily became aware of black kids materializing out of the distant pecan trees. Eight or nine boys and girls, little brothers and sisters tagging along, were suddenly standing there, waiting for us to invite them to play.

"Y'all come on out," Bubba called.

"Y'all want to get up a game?" I said, tossing up the ball and hitting one to Billy in center field. When he missed it, Skip retrieved it for him, dropping the ball from his mouth in front of Billy.

When I glanced around, the black kids were now standing about twenty paces closer. I'd hardly seen them move. When they saw me looking at them, the little kids fell to wrestling self-consciously and scuffling with each other, rolling on the ground and kicking up tiny clouds of dust. They were wearing grimy, scruffy clothes that looked made for midgets. Eventually the biggest boy sidled up to me. I'd seen him before, but I didn't remember his name.

"I'm Ollie," he said.

"Hey, Ollie, I'm Willie. Ollie what?"

"Caruthers. Willie what?"

"Morris."

We appraised each other, looking each other up and down like hunters squinting out from the brush. He gestured toward his companions. "And he's Navy and he's Reginald and that's my little brother, Oscar."

Ollie and I continued to size each other up. We were about the same age. He wasn't black but the smooth rich color of milk chocolate. He was both foreign and not. I felt a divide between us, but then again, I didn't. He wore a grey T-shirt

and grimy khaki men's workpants that had been cut down in the legs. They were too big for him in the waist and were cinched tight with a piece of cord. The frayed bottoms flapped around his bare feet when he kicked at the dust. He saw me looking at his clothes and crossed his arms defensively. Behind him, his friends crossed their arms, too.

"Is that yo' *glove?*" he said disdainfully. My Rawlings baseball glove was lying on the ground beside me.

"Want to try it?" I said. "Go ahead."

He picked it up and slid his hand inside. When he pounded the pocket, his eyes lit up.

"That's all right," he said.

I thought, *I've got an old glove at home I don't use any more.*

"Y'all ready to play?" I said.

"Yeah," he said.

"Want to walk off the bases?"

"All right, we can use them sticks there for home plate and first, second, and third," he said.

Everybody got busy setting up a baseball diamond. The black kids had one more player than we did, not counting the little brothers and sisters who sat near the sideline silently watching us in all our gyrations, but that didn't matter. We agreed that their extra player would catch for both sides. They could bat first and use our gloves when we were at bat.

I started pitching, not throwing hard, giving them a chance to get into the rhythm. It felt good standing there in the warm stirring breeze from the river, the soft, tender cloud banks drifting lambently on the horizon, the town itself etched against its slow, descending bluffs. At first they swung wildly at every pitch, reaching for outside balls, and low ones, and striking out. But it didn't take the one named Ollie long to start hitting. He was a good natural athlete, a fast baserunner and quick fielder. I wished we had him on our team at school. After two innings, the score was 3–0 in our favor. They didn't seem to notice the score, or if they did, they didn't let on.

The next time Ollie came to bat, I decided to try out the curveball Daddy taught me. I wrapped two fingers along the stitches, the way I'd been instructed, snapped my wrist, and let fly. It broke sharply just before it crossed home plate. Ollie saw the ball coming at him and stepped away before it broke. His brother Oscar, who was catching for both teams, missed the catch and had to scramble after the ball.

"That was a *curve*," Ollie said.

"Never seen one before?" I called.

"Naw, throw me another one."

I saw him set himself to stand in against the curve. This time I threw a better breaking ball, a long, slow curve that tingled my wrist and sent little electric pulsations up my funny bone. "Don't throw many of them at your age," Daddy always said. "You'll throw out your arm. When your funny bone tingles, don't throw no more yet." Ollie stepped into it and hit a strong line drive far over Bubba's head at second base. By the time Henjie ran it down in the weeds, Ollie had nearly rounded third base, his bare feet slapping the ground like thudding drumbeats. I covered home, pounding my glove and yelling for Henjie to throw it to me. All the little brothers and sisters were jumping up and down. Henjie's throw was a perfect one-hopper that I snagged near what would've been the baseline just as Ollie started to slide headfirst. We both dived toward the stick at the same time. I was sure I touched his leg with the ball before his hand found the stick. We sat together in a petulant cloud of dust.

"Safe!" Ollie cried, and looked at me with dusty brown eyebrows raised.

"Yeah, safe," I said. "Good hit."

"Naw, you tagged him out!" Bubba shouted. The black children grew quiet, watching and waiting.

"Tie goes to the runner," I said. "He's safe."

We played for a while longer, maybe an hour, maybe two. Nobody had a watch and time didn't matter, anyway, because the days were like that then. Then one of Ollie's friends had to take his little brothers home, and the game swiftly broke up. Ollie and I sat on the ground, chewing blades of grass and feeling a little friendly and relaxed.

"You're a good ball player," I said.

"I can hit your curve ball," he replied.

"Wait till I work on it," I said. "You ain't seen nothin' yet."

"I can still hit it."

"I got another ball glove at home," I said, then regretted it, not knowing my own regret.

Football

North Toward Starkville

MEMOIR

as we grow older, is often damaging. But this was one of the Lord's good days, resting for me forever in a kind of somnolent tenderness. I was thirteen, and on a golden, luminous November afternoon I was to see my first Ole Miss-Mississippi State game in person.

My emotions were ambivalent. I was a Yazoo City boy. As Yazoo was half Delta and half hills, it was also half Ole Miss and half Mississippi State, and remains so to this day: a most schizophrenic locale. I loved both teams. I was partial to the Mississippi State Maroons because the noble, distinguished running back Shorty McWilliams's sister lived across the street from my childhood house on Grand Avenue in Yazoo. "Shorty Mac," of Meridian, Mississippi, whom we knew then in almost quintessential reverence, had played in the same backfield with the legendary Glenn Davis and Doc Blanchard at West Point, the U. S. Military Academy, in those halcyon wartime days, the latter ones when we were whipping the Germans and the Japs, then returned for his final season at his beloved State.

When Shorty Mac visited his sister and brother-in-law across from my house in Yazoo City, he would come over and play touch football in my front yard with Jimmy Ball, Bubba Barrier, Bee Barrier, Jerry Barrier, Buford Atkinson, Henjie Henick, many Graeber, Nicholas and Barbour boys, Art "Worms" Doty, my dog Skip, and myself. Then he'd sit around with us on my front porch and tell football stories, gingerly tossing the football in his lap, tousling our hair and calling us by specific name. All of us, Yazoo boys, girls and dogs, were enthralled with the ineffable Shorty Mac, and we still owe him much.

Yet I had another hero, too, who made my growing-up days of football fealty dislocated—the unforgettable Charlie Conerly of Ole Miss. I listened glowingly on the radio to Conerly's indelible touchdown passes to Barney Poole, who had also played on the same good old army team with Shorty Mac, Blanchard and Davis, before returning, as had Shorty Mac, for his last season in his native Mississippi.

Back in those days, in Mississippi in the 1940s, it was a lengthy winding drive from Yazoo City to Oxford or Starkville. This was long before Eisenhower's federal interstates, and one had intimate private glimpses of the little isolated towns along the way, and the people who dwelled in them, and the solitary exultant Saturday mystery of them, the wonderful Saturday freedom of their wan lost facades. The drives to the State-Ole Miss games at Oxford or Starkville were enveloped in the beauty of the Deep South's autumns. Mississippi has never had the great flamboyant bursting beauty of New England autumns, but there is a languor to our Novembers, especially in the dry falls when the foliage is so profound and varied, and the very landscape itself is suffused with a warm, golden, poignant patina. And that is the way I wish to remember this especial drive to the State-Ole Miss game of 1947, and those with us in the Pontiac on that day, most now long dead, buried under mimosas in the Yazoo cemetery in the last sloping reluctant foothills before the Delta.

We drove up from Yazoo City toward Starkville on that forenoon in a faraway boyhood. We had to go north through the Delta on No. 49-E along the grey, precipitous bluffs, then east on No. 82. There were no McDonald's or Wendy's or Sonic's then either, but Mrs. Nel Barrier had made us fried chicken and deviled eggs and innumerable pimento and pineapple and peanut butter and cucumber sandwiches for this odyssey—and added six Moonpies and a dozen R. C.'s for good measure.

I was with my ancient comrade, Bubba Barrier, whom I'd grown up with since age two, Bubba's father Hibbie who had been an Ole Miss Rebel halfback in the

1920s and was my surrogate father, and Mr. Hibbie's best friend whom I shall call Wade "Quail" Hampton, a car salesman in Yazoo long since gone as is Mr. Hibbie to the great Ole Miss-State game in the sky. Mr. "Quail" did not turn to the sour mash until Tchula on this morning, but by Winona he knew little of mortal earthy anguish.

And then the tableau at the lovely Scott Field on this warm, cloudless day: both clubs 7–2, twenty-five thousand rabid souls, and the two all-Americans, Shorty Mac and Charlie. And in the grandstand watching, Shorty Mac's and Barney Poole's old teammate from the immortal Black Knights of the Hudson, Glenn Davis!

Charlie, a Marine hero in the South Pacific who had known death and mayhem in World War II, much more than any opposing football team ever could wreak, had set a new national passing record of 120 completions before this game, only the second collegian in history to pass for more than 100 in one year. His swift, arching passes, with their drama and deft synchronism, were resonant and imperishable as a Wagnerian chorus, and were national institutions. Barney Poole, in his seventh year of college football (he was rumored to be forty-one), broke a national record that afternoon for pass receptions.

It was an Ole Miss day, this one. Halfway through the first quarter, the Rebels' Buddy Bowen sneaked over the goal line from the 3-yard line right in front of us in the south end zone, precisely at the moment Mr. Wade "Quail" Hampton fell out of the eighth-row end-zone seat onto the grass. Bubba and I revived him with a wet handkerchief during the extra-point conversion, kneeling near him like mendicants before a stricken warrior, which got Mr. "Quail" into the third quarter.

Shorty Mac was carried off with an injury, and Charlie Conerly was unerring. At one juncture he completed eleven straight passes, usually to the mucilaginous-fingered Barney Poole. The Rebels were using the old Notre Dame Box under Johnny Vaught. I remember as if yesterday Charlie falling on his back, yet throwing the ball fifty yards unencumbered in the air to Joe Johnson, who tenderly gathered it in on the 15, losing his shoe to a Maroon named Eagle Matulich and striding into the end zone barefooted. At this point Mr. "Quail" Hampton was passed out in Bubba's lap and would not be revived until east of Eden on the way home.

Their names on both sides were Hairline Harper, Oscar Buchanan (later our high school football coach in Yazoo), Farley Salmon, Dub Garrett, Will Glover, Bill Erickson, Jack Odom, Max Stenibrook, Eulas "Red" Jenkins—and of course Shorty Mac and Charlie. Some of them are dead now also.

That was forty-five years ago, at Scott Field in Starkville, but I still see now Joe Johnson taking Charlie's long pass into the end zone without his shoe, in front of Mr. Hibbie, Mr. "Quail," Bubba and me.

Even as a grown man, I still root for State in every game every year except one, and despite my friend "Dog" Brewer, the Ole Miss coach, I might be for the Maroons next game if they still had good, old, fine Shorty Mac.

Cheerleaders vs. Baton Twirlers

M E M O I R

It was

a clear, warm night of late September in Harpole Stadium. The signs on the visitors' side proclaimed: TAME THE TORNADOES!, COUGAR BLITZ!, and BITE THE DUST, MARCUS! Northwest Rankin, half white and half black, had only twenty-eight on its traveling squad, including a substitute end who weighed 122 pounds, and its band wore matching T-shirts and trousers.

Earlier in the day, at the Downtown Hotel in Philadelphia, I had arranged to meet two friends who had driven from Oxford. Both were intrepid followers of football. Russell Blair, known as "The Commander," was a lawyer who had played sports at Annapolis in the late thirties and was on the U.S.S. *California* at Pearl Harbor on December 7, 1941. Charles Henry was an insurance man, a Deltan who had grown up on the Coldwater River between Sledge and Darling. Commander Blair and Charles Henry were curious to observe Marcus for the first time.

There was no scoring in the first quarter. Marcus had runs of four, six, seven, eight, nine, and twelve yards. Early in the second quarter he broke off tackle out of the Wishbone for a fourteen-yard touchdown. Less than two minutes later Mark Burnside scored from forty-one yards out to put Philly in front, 12–0. Marcus, directing the kickoff team with timing signals, came over to the sidelines and raised his arms to solicit yells from the home crowd. The fans stood in unison, clapping and shouting.

He was gaining substantial yardage. My companions from Oxford expressed their pleasure with terse, clipped comments and an occasional flamboyant oath. Then he headed up the middle on a long run. Number 10 of the Northwest Rankin Cougars, whose name was Jessie Bilbro, caught him by the shirt and the top of his football trousers and held on with great tenacity. Marcus pulled him another ten yards, but Bilbro refused to let go, sliding along on the ground until two of his teammates finally made the tackle after a fifty-two-yard gain. This unusual feat was a little like mixing sex with booze; it was not poetic, but it worked. The home crowd laughed, then applauded young Bilbro's accomplishment in a spirit of sportsmanship. The Navy's Blair and the insurance man Henry were equally impressed. "Number 10 will remember when he's an old man," one of them said, "holdin' on to Marcus Dupree's shirt like a man holdin' on to a wild mule." A little later, with 5:33 remaining in the first half, he ran over half a dozen defenders, including the indomitable Jessie Bilbro, on a forty-seven-yard sweep for a touchdown. Philly 19, Northwest Rankin 0.

Every halftime all year, as was my habit, I wandered about the stadium chatting with Principal Gregory, "Boots" Howell, Superintendent Myers, young Amy Kilpatrick, and others, to the strains of the Philadelphia band, which performed "New York, New York," addressing itself to making it big in the city that does not sleep. The band played "New York, New York" each halftime that whole season, so that I knew its every note in my heart.

The homecoming queen and maids were then presented. The white and black girls were escorted to the center of the field by their fathers as the voice on the loudspeaker made the introductions. "First in our line of royalty is maid-at-large Betty Hampton." There was general applause. She was a black girl in a yellow evening dress, and she was cited as a member of the Society of Distinguished American High School Students. Another black girl, Teresa Stribling, was introduced as president of the senior class, five-year honor student, and "most intellectual girl" her senior year. Similar homage was paid to the other beaming girls of both races in the Tornado court of royalty.

During these ceremonies, merely in the mood of casual inquiry, I walked over to the visitors' side of the field. The cheerleaders of the visiting team and of Philadelphia had congregated in a little semicircle near the empty players' bench to exchange the traditional felicities. And with this I must be indulged a brief digression of the most academic nature.

I immediately took notice of one of the visitors' cheerleaders. She was so stunningly beautiful that the sight of her was like a sudden blow in the back of the neck. She stood there among her fellows in a pose of studied nonchalance; I knew she was very aware of her beauty. She was one of those willowy blond lovelies in whom the sovereign state of Mississippi had forever abounded and been justly famous. Her soft, clean features stood out in the festive Neshoba evening. Without warning, in that instant, I was overcome with an emotion of sadness. What would become of this splendid young creature? Where might she be twenty years from this night? In the suburbia of Greater Atlanta or Memphis or Birmingham? On the field the Philadelphia band was playing again:

> *My little town blues*
> *Are melting away,*
> *I'll make a brand new start of it*
> *In old New York . . .*

Would she have a long, happy life? Surely she would not grow old and die! As she detached herself momentarily from her companions, for little reason at all she performed a ginger cartwheel, then a tender arabesque. I sensed as I always had the worm in the lilac, remembering anew the lines of Emily Dickinson:

> *This quiet Dust was Gentlemen and Ladies*
> *And Lads and Girls—*
> *Was laughter and ability and Sighing,*
> *And Frocks and Curls.*

She returned to the friendly semicircle. She looked up into the bleachers, tossing back her long golden hair. Behind me some county fellows in Coors T-shirts and tractor caps were snickering about her. "She is one of those village beauties of which the South is so prodigal," Walker Percy said in *The Moviegoer* about Binx Bolling's secretary in New Orleans from Eufala, Alabama. "No one marvels at them; no one holds them dear. They flush out of their nests first thing and alight in the cities to stay, and no one misses them. Even their men pay no attention to them, any way far less attention than they pay to money. But I marvel at them; I miss them; I hold them dear." Binx Bolling marveled likewise that, twenty years ago, "practically every other girl born in Gentilly must have been named Marcia. A year or so later it was Linda. Then Sharon. In recent years I have noted that the name Stephanie has come into fashion."

Had only Binx Bolling been with me in my travels in that imperishable autumn of 1981 to the high school football stadia of east-central Mississippi studying the cheerleaders. Philadelphia itself had *Stephanie* Griffin, as well as *Yvonne* Burnette, *Dee Dee* Morgan, *Tonya* Alexander, *Suzette* Black, *Rhonda* Allen, and *Lori* Sharp. I would not, unfortunately, match the black or white faces with the names, but 1964 must have been an auspicious year for Europe, and especially France. Might Jacqueline Kennedy have had an influence here? Eupora featured *Jacqueline* Gary and *Corinne* Hooper, Newton had *Denise* Cumberland, and in time I would see and admire *Denise* LeFlore of Carthage and *Renee* Thompson of New Hope. My favorites included *Falisia* Fullilove of Winona, *Nina* Glaze and *Sonya* Bounds of Newton, and *Vonda* Bowie and *Angel* Stephenson of Ackerman. Otherwise the rosters would include *Misti, Christi, Lori, Terri, Sherri, Wendi, Vicky,* and *Cindi; Cissy, Starry, Tammy,* and *Sandy; Debbie, Berdie,* and *Connie;* two *Pams,* a *Malissa* and a *Melissa;* and one each of the more utilitarian *Sharron, Dorice, Tina, Kim, Ilean,* and *Jimmie Lyn.* God bless them every one.

"High school football games are great for fathers of teenaged daughters who are cheerleaders," a father of just such a cheerleader in Oxford, Mississippi, had told me. "Teenaged daughters love to scream. This gets them out of the house to scream, and in a good cause." He produced for me his cheerleader-daughter's shopping list before the first game of the season, done in her own hand:

> 1 nautical blue eyeliner
> 1 shell white eyeshadow
> 1 Burgundy Blush
> 1 Cinnamon Blush (Covergirl)
> 1 Plum Berry Blush (Revlon)

"The 'Blushes,' you see, are like rouge," he explained to me. "She's been experimenting before the games."

Throughout the season, as I followed the fortunes of the noble Marcus Dupree, I discovered that the styles of all the cheerleaders in the various towns, when placed under rigorous scrutiny, seemed rather similar. This led one to suspect that most of them had attended the Ole Miss Cheerleaders' Clinic in the summer. Strolling across that campus one afternoon the previous July, I had been exposed to the most bizarre spectacle—a scene from Fellini. Walking up the street or through the Grove toward their mass convocations, the cheer-

leaders from each school would be clustered together, wearing their school colors. As they strolled along they were practicing their favorite or most difficult yells. One group of little nymphets in matching blue and gold were actually perched in the limbs of an elm tree doing their routines. Another was on the roof of a sorority house. Some of the squads were half white and half black. Others had only one or two black girls in their number. I counted one group with ten blacks and two whites. Several were all white—the private academies, no doubt, from Jackson or the Delta. Imagine, if you will, regardless of your sociological bias, walking innocently across the Ole Miss campus with your beloved dog Pete, and then being bombarded from every direction by hundreds upon hundreds of screaming teenagers, strutting to various beats, yelling their different yells in the fashionable black cadences, one battalion of them disappearing down the hill while another—echoing from the distance—appears suddenly from around a bend, more arduous than the one before.

The next week, one knew, the high school twirlers would arrive for the Ole Miss Baton Twirling Clinic. The twirlers would be quieter, more sedate. But there were other differences as well, almost existential in substance. As I stood on the North Rankin side of the Philadelphia stadium at halftime on this night, investigating the cheerleaders of both teams, I remembered what an especially perspicacious law student had told me not many days before. "Baton twirlers are more thoughtful and deliberative," he had explained. "I believe they have a more lonely calling than cheerleaders. In the South, and especially in Mississippi, many of the twirlers' mothers were twirlers. That's an unconscionable burden, you know. The mothers get their daughters started in twirling at an early age. They want to relive their own youth as twirlers through their daughters. How often do you see that among cheerleaders? One girl I know of—her mother was a twirler in the 1950s at Copiah-Lincoln Junior College, they called them 'Co-Letts'—started twirling when she was two or three years old. She was the featured twirler at Brookhaven High School and later tried out for the main job at Southern Mississippi. She didn't make it. It was sad."

My advisor continued: "Cheerleaders don't suffer the way twirlers do. Twirlers aren't in a group all the time. They're the last of the individualists. But it's all changing. The trend now is toward a drum-and-bugle-corps style, twirling rifles and flags and God knows what else. It's the damned Pentagon influence. The individual twirler is out now in Mississippi, but who knows? Toynbee had it right. Twirling comes and goes in cycles." I appreciated the law student's wise counsel. From that night I began to look on both professions with a new eye.

The Fumble

F I C T I O N

we were in the seventh grade, school superintendent Loren P. Ledbetter did something unbelievable. He put Central High of Jackson on our football schedule for a game five years in the future, compounding the blasphemy by agreeing to play in Jackson. Old Man Ledbetter was strange anyway, and left school three years after that with a vague shadow on his name, but the damage had been done. I remember the afternoon everyone heard what he had gotten us into. "He's lost his marbles," Mr. Chris Wesley told a group of merchants while cutting my hair. "He's crazy as a swamp bird." They all shook their heads. "Jackson Central!"

We were a town of seven thousand, half of them colored, sixty miles north of Jackson, a poor little town of undistinguished facades perched there on the banks of our murky river, while Jackson was the capital of Mississippi. It was a brisk metropolis of well over one hundred thousand citizens with swimming pools and country clubs and mansions with pickaninny statues on the lush lawns and hotels twenty stories high with nightclubs on top which let people bring their own whiskey, and everything touched a little with the Yankee dollar. "The Crossroads of the South," its signs proclaimed. Our families drove all the way to Jackson to shop in Kennington's or The Emporium on Capitol Street, or to take us to the zoo. Central High was the only white high school in the whole city. Its majestic school buildings were right around the corner from the Capitol and the Governor's Mansion and covered an entire block, a dominion unto itself, self-assured and expansive as any university. We knew all about the Central High Tigers as far back as grammar school. They had seventy-five boys or more on their football team and once won thirty-two games in a row, playing in the fabulous Big Eight Conference. Their best players went on to Ole Miss, where they joined SAE or KA and got the reigning Delta beauties, then moved successfully into brokerage or real estate, usually in Memphis or Atlanta. Our school, given its size, could barely get thirty boys together and played in the lowly Delta Valley Conference against other little towns out in the flat cotton country.

Shortly after the word got out, Billy Bonner and I were walking down the street toward his house, avoiding the cracks in the sidewalk as was our habit.

"They scheduled us for a *breather*," Billy said suddenly, for Mr. Ledbetter's folly had been worrying him all afternoon. Billy's father, who was the Chevrolet dealer, had once taken us to a game in Jackson. Fifteen thousand people came to those games in the fancy stadium off State Street! And not only from Jackson but from all over middle Mississippi, just to watch the unfolding of the invincible.

Billy paused a moment, then added as if in revelation: "That game's in five years, right? We'll be seniors."

I recall the exact moment Billy said that, because it was a dark, gloomy day of intermittent rain, and a clap of thunder rolled out of the hills, and Mr. Son Graham standing in front of the funeral home dropped a Seven-Up bottle.

The seasons drifted by. I grew six inches between the tenth and eleventh grades, and people claimed I was growing so fast I buzzed like a bee. We learned how to kiss and fondle the beautiful girls in the back seats of cars, which we parked near the cemetery or out beyond the Illinois Central tracks in the Delta side of town. We stopped going to Sunday school. We drove into the hills and found a surreptitious clearing which we had almost forgotten from our childhood and drank ice-cold beer and smoked cigarettes. The town boys had grown up together and went around in a group. Bubba Poindexter. Billy Bonner. Hershell Meade. Ed Wilburn Walters. Cotton Simmons. Kayo Fentress. "Hans" Weems. Our girls were the town girls from the best old families.

I mentioned that the town was poor. That is only partly true. We were Delta people and depended on cotton, so the town was poor one year and rich the next, and everything pertained to mortgage. The planters lived in fine houses in town and rode out to their land every day in khakis like hired hands. One thunderstorm too many, or three days without rain at a critical moment, could be disastrous. That was why the talk of the weather was not a social form but an obsession, for our people were gamblers against the eternal elements. The young people from the country who came to school from out of the hills were poor. The hill-country boys made good tackles and guards and centers. The town boys were backs and ends, and the town girls were majorettes and cheerleaders. I would not have used the word then, but we all had pride. It was a quirky-proud town.

One afternoon when I was fifteen I was sitting alone at the counter of the drug store after a movie—*To Have and Have Not*, with Humphrey Bogart and Lauren Bacall. It was the middle of the summer and the drug store was somnolent as the town. All of a sudden two cars parked in front. One was a new Buick sedan, the other a new Oldsmobile convertible. I noticed the big decals on both cars etched in black and gold, which said: "Jackson Central High." Four couples of high school age came inside. The boys lorded it all over the country girl who worked at the soda fountain. They were expensively dressed in the casual southern way. The girls wore shiny shorts and tight blouses and flitted around the jukebox, pouring in a mountain of nickels.

"Play some Tony Bennett!" one of the boys shouted from the counter.

"Hell no, play some Nat King Cole!" another demanded. I recognized him. I had seen his picture several times in the sports section of the Jackson *Daily News*. He was a tailback.

From the mirror I saw them sit down at a table, where they drank their cherry cokes and whispered fun of the people who drifted in and out of the drug store. Then they ordered milkshakes, and hot dogs, and onion rings, and kept putting nickels in the jukebox. Eventually they got up to leave. They started to stroll down main street. I followed at a discreet distance.

"What a funny little town," one of the girls said. I hated her golden beauty, her honeyed hair.

Then they returned to their cars. I stood alone under the shade of the awning of Mr. "Chewing Gum" Fulgate's tire store watching them. Mr. Fulgate joined me. "Who are them kids?" he asked.

"They're from Jackson Central High," I said.

"Damned snobs!"

One of the boys threw a balled-up chewing gum wrapper at an old colored man who was propped asleep against the side of Jitney Jungle. Then the two cars disappeared around Broadway.

I saw the same tailback again on a Friday afternoon that fall. It was one of those cool, windswept days of late October, and Billy Bonner and Bubba Poindexter and I were waiting in the service station at the top of Broadway while they repaired the water pump on Billy's old robin's-egg blue Chevy. Three bright new buses pulled in for gas, painted in black and gold with "Central High of Jackson" on their sides.

"They're headed into the Delta," Billy said. "They're playing Greenville tonight."

As the buses departed, I saw the tailback sitting on the front row of one of them. He and his friends looked down at us. They grinned and gave us the finger.

Our senior year arrived soon enough. I remember the news from Korea on the radio.

That year they brought in a new football coach. His name was "Blackie" Piersall, a big chunky young man who had played with Charlie Conerly, Barney Poole, and Farley Salmon at Ole Miss. The first thing he did was install the Split-T formation.

In my junior year I had made the travelling squad under Coach "Aussie" Austin, who wore glasses and had three fingers on his left hand, but I failed to earn a letter. I was the third-team wingback in the single-wing offense and only got in on seven plays all season. We finished with two wins and eight losses, including a 50–7 debacle at the hands of Belzoni, and they got rid of Aussie Austin, whose reputation in his three years was for cursing at his players with florid, unheard-of four-letter words and for paying too much attention to the girls in his forestry class. He had also broken out a window of our dressing room with a football shoe after our 20–0 loss to Indianola.

Despite the fact that he sang bass in the Episcopal choir, Coach Blackie Piersall was a rigid taskmaster. During our torrid two-a-day practices late that summer at Poindexter Field, as we suffocated in the 100-degree heat and ran our interminable wind sprints, he told us this would be "The Year of the Choctaws." I would go home at sunset and sit for a long time in a hot bath, nursing my bruises and drinking gallons of water.

"Did you drink a lot of water when you got home yesterday?" he once asked me.

"No sir," I lied.

"Well, don't do it. Water's no good for you in this weather."

"You fellows are used to the single-wing," he lectured us right at the start. "The Split-T's a whole new ball game. It's revolutionized a slow old sport. It's designed for a small, quick, run-oriented offense. It don't give you much time. You gotta be quick, quick! Don't tarry. Move around at all times." And with that he would send us off on ten more wind sprints in the broiling dust.

Even before school opened, Central High of Jackson loomed before us, a monstrous negation of our hopes. It would be our ninth game, the next-to-last one. As the season began, we read every Saturday in the supercilious Jackson papers of the exploits of the Central Tigers. By the time of our first game, against Indianola at home, I was the second-team right halfback behind Billy Bonner. We lost to Indianola, 21–14, under the pale lights of our field before two thousand spectators and three million Delta bugs who were drawn in out of the bottoms by the illumination, while Jackson Central was destroying Natchez, 48–0. "A big cat playing around with a little mouse," the Jackson papers said of Jackson Central High and Natchez, not only ignoring the fact that Natchez had humiliated Belzoni 60–12 in the same year Belzoni beat us 50–7, but ignoring too the noble and patrician history of that city by the river, which I had read about in a book loaned to me by Mrs. Idella King and called *The Old Natchez Lineage* by Priscilla Jumper Tankersly.

I did not even play in that first game. I was skinny, six feet and 150 pounds, and people made fun of my legs. I was the third fastest member of the squad, behind Billy Bonner and Bubba Poindexter, but I could not knock down a toothpick. Yet it was not merely the thing to do to be on that team, even though I was not especially good at it. More than ritual was at stake. There was the matter of duty and honor, although I did not perceive it that way in those days, of course.

Oh, but I remember that golden Indian summer, and the delicious, bittersweet throbs of love—Katie Culpepper, a long-legged majorette, sweet and cheery and lush, a fount of loyalty and fun. I had just won the high school spelling bee, a marathon that lasted six straight weekly assemblies, culminating in a lengthy *mano a mano* with Marion Whittington which put everyone to sleep until, after two hours and twenty minutes, as we lobbed words back and forth between us as lazily as tennis balls on a summer's day, a subtle electricity seized the atmosphere of the auditorium and all the bored boys and girls in the flush of creamy Mississippi adolescence suddenly opened their eyes and stirred to life when Mrs. Idella King pronounced the word *sacrilegious*. Divine irony intervened

when I snared Marion Whittington, son of a pastor, on just such a word. I believe even Coach Blackie Piersall was impressed.

And so was Katie Culpepper, who hugged me right in the hallway outside the auditorium and whispered: "My darling boy." Katie, who would go anywhere and do anything—sit with me on her front porch and watch the cars go by, or play me her records, or drive the backroads on smoky afternoons, or dance close to the words of Jo Stafford with her fingers casually on the lobe of my ear, or ask if I was happy and what could she do to make me happier, or explain to me why she was a connoisseur of Dr. Peppers and strawberry milkshakes, or study her books with me on school evenings and ask for help. . . . Katie, my straight-C scholar of deep embraces and warm moist kisses, a childlike face and woman's hips and full ripe breasts that became mine long before that long-ago night against Central High of Jackson.

Leaves of a dozen colors drifted down out of the trees in those sad and wistful days, those sad, horny Delta days. We remember what we wish to remember; it is all there to be summoned, but we pick and choose—since we are what we are—as we must and will. Katie and I are standing in the side lawn of her house, under an ancient water chestnut. She had been showing me her baton twirling tricks, picked up at the Ole Miss Baton Twirling Clinic. She is still tanned from the summer sun, her long blond hair is bobbed at the back, and her green eyes twinkle in mirth. I lean across and kiss her gently on the lips, and she kisses me in return. We stand in a light, amiable embrace; her cheek brushes mine. Oh, sweet agony of the loins! Bubba and Billy suddenly speed by in Billy's Chevy, Debbie and Laura Jane in tow, and shout greetings at us, and the leaves arc aimlessly from the trees, and there is a hazy crispness in the air. I gaze down from the summit of a quarter of a century, living in the Kingdom of the Yankee, all the accumulated losses and guilts and shames and rages, the loves come and gone, and *death*, ravenous death, and I summon now that instant standing in the shade of the chestnut with Katie Culpepper, herself long dead, buried under a mimosa on the hill in our cemetery far away, and I am caught ever so briefly in a frieze of old time, skinny and tall and seventeen, and the senior year stretching before me as a Lewis Carroll dream, beckoning: "Come, lad."

Artifice, all of it. They were burying the Korean dead. And Jackson Central two months away.

The next week, again at home, we edged Leland, 14–13, to the margin of Hershell Meade's extra points, as I acquired splinters on the bench and Bubba

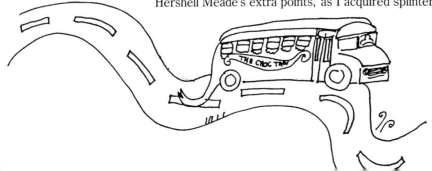

Poindexter ran eighty-two yards for one touchdown and thirty-six for another with college scouts in the grandstand. However, the grizzly and prematurely aging country boys in our line would not block, and the band played off key. We got our senior rings that day, and at the dance after the game I gave mine to Katie, who put adhesive tape on the inside and wore it on her index finger.

That next Friday we were on the road against Belzoni, a tough cotton hamlet forty miles into the Delta, a cotton-gin and honky-tonk town nestled on the same saturnine river as ours. I should describe this road trip in some detail, not only because it was a small presage of things to come, but because I learned something from it, one of those life's lessons a young man is supposed to get from football, as Coach Blackie Piersall and everyone else said.

We had a rickety old bus, painted in our colors, red and black, with "The Choctaw" on both sides. That Friday afternoon we boarded The Choctaw in front of the school building. The students came out to send us off. The band played the fight song, which Notre Dame University had stolen from us, and the cheerleaders and majorettes pirouetted under the somber skies. They would all follow us into the flat land later in the day. I waved goodby to Katie, and with a rattle of gears we were off to the Tenderloin Grill at the top of the hill for a pre-game meal of roast beef and mashed potatoes.

No sooner had we gotten on The Choctaw again than it began to rain, a hard relentless Mississippi rain that would not stop for a long time.

It certainly had not stopped well into the third quarter against the rugged, sinister Belzoni boys before twelve or fourteen hundred drenched spectators on the field behind their school. I sat on the edge of the bench under an umbrella Katie had brought me from the bleachers, sharing it with Gene Autry Simms, our second-team guard. Although the Belzonians had already lost their first two games, they were unyielding against us as always, and they weighed two hundred pounds from tackle to tackle. I was ashamed of my clean uniform. The Belzoni fans shouted curses at my comrades toiling in the precarious mud of that field, ignoring Gene Autry and me.

A succession of disasters struck in that quarter. Billy Bonner fractured his little finger, but Blackie Piersall kept him in. Cotton Simmons, the right end, took an underhanded blow to the lip and was led off with a mouth the size of a grapefruit. He was treated by Dr. Tommy Gilruth, who came and sat next to him on the bench and asked him what day it was. Cotton later told us he did not know what *state* we were in, so much for the day. Ed Wilburn Walters sprained his ankle on a pass pattern in the flat. Hans Weems, substituting for Ed

Wilburn, was cleated in the neck. Kayo Fentress was knocked unconscious by a gang tackle and did not wake up until the fourth quarter. Big Ruby Mitchell broke his nose and was replaced at fullback by Juice Coody. Leroy Hipps, our biggest man at tackle (later second-team all-Southeastern Conference at Mississippi State) broke two fingers on two different plays. Everyone else on that filthy, moiling turf sustained bad bruises in the quarter, and there was blood mixed in with the Delta ooze. On the bench I smeared some of the mud on my jersey. At that moment the loudspeaker gave some outside scores. Jackson Central 53, Biloxi 12.

And it was close. With three minutes remaining in the game Belzoni was ahead 19–14, but we had the ball at midfield. A Belzoni partisan threw a bottle toward our huddle and was led away by two state troopers. Our band broke into the fight song.

Suddenly Billy Bonner staggered to our bench with a gash on his elbow. Blackie Piersall motioned to me. I threw down my umbrella as he yanked me by the arm. "Tell Hershell 'Tear Left.'" There was a strange glint in his eye.

I raced onto the field, almost slipping in the mud, and gave the play to Hershell Meade. "Tear Left" was a quick pitch to Bubba Poindexter at left halfback, with the left tackle, Leroy Hipps, leading interference around left end and the right halfback—myself—feinting into the line. Our flanker, Hans Weems, went in motion to the right and the fullback, Juice Coody, filled the hole where Leroy pulled. If Hans did a good job hookblocking the defensive end, we had a chance for long yardage. As I hit a tangle of Belzoni linemen, I heard a roar from our side of the field. Bubba picked up his blockers and gained eighteen yards to the Belzoni 32-yard line. In the huddle Hershell called the same play. This time Bubba went to the 24. Second and two, two minutes ten seconds to play.

Billy Bonner appeared from nowhere in the huddle and pulled at my jersey. Dr. Gilruth had poured iodine on his cut, and so much for me. I ran off the field and got my umbrella back from Gene Autry Simms. I felt a drop of blood on my cheek. I allowed it to stay there.

Billy Bonner straight ahead for seven. First and ten on the Belzoni 17. Juice Coody up the middle for three. Second and seven on the 14. One minute, twenty-seven seconds. Bubba Poindexter on the pitchout option for six. Third and one on the 8. Bubba on the quick-opener for three. First and goal on the 5.

Through the mist and rain the bedraggled scoreboard showed forty-seven seconds to play. Billy Bonner for one on the right side. Bubba Poindexter for one on the quick-opener. Third and goal from the three. Fourteen seconds to play.

Hershell Meade called time out. Blackie Piersall shouted for Gene Autry Simms. We all crowded around in the rain to listen. "56-B, end zone buttonhook, got it, Gene Autry? *Got it, Gene Autry?*" Coach Piersall sometimes complained that Gene Autry forgot the plays between the bench and the huddle. Gene Autry, who stuttered, nodded his big head and entered the battle.

Our cheerleaders were soggy silhouettes as they gazed out onto the field. Mr. "Chewing Gum" Fulgate, sitting in the middle of a group of merchants, seemed in an attitude of prayer. The high school principal, Mr. Terry Buffaloe, had both arms raised with his fists clenched, and Mrs. Buffaloe was hiding her eyes with her hands.

We broke from the huddle, Hershell Meade barking the signals. Hershell faded back with the snap. There, as sweet and effortless as a Mozart minuet, all alone a few yards deep into the end zone on the buttonhook, was Billy Bonner. An easy lob by Hershell, and Billy had it. Four seconds to play, 20–19. Hershell booted the conversion, Belzoni went nowhere on the final kickoff, and that was it.

I have failed to explain that Coach Blackie Piersall was gentler than he seemed. In fact, as the season progressed, perhaps out of our mutual adversity, he actually grew more kind-hearted, and even more intelligent. Normally he would have let our girls, the majorettes and cheerleaders, ride back home with us on The Choctaw. But everyone was too hurt for that. After we had dressed in near stony silence in the dreary visitors' locker room populated by roaches, we limped onto the bus. I rolled down my window and took Katie's hand. The other girls flocked around the faithful Choctaw, cooing to the wounded: "Good game, Billy . . . Good game Hershell . . . Good game, Ed Wilburn." "Good game," Katie said, and blew me a fine kiss.

As Blackie Piersall started the motor and Dr. Tommy Gilruth handed out aspirin, I noticed Billy Bonner reaching outside his window for a sizeable object. Billy's daddy was handing him up a case of beer.

Blackie Piersall also saw this, but said nothing, as Billy distributed the sweet nectar of Jax to his teammates. The bus rattled through the desolate streets of Belzoni and onto the flat, straight highway home. Except for a few moans and short, clipped curses, no one said much of anything. Cotton Simmons's mouth, though the swelling had subsided, looked ghastly. Kayo Fentress appeared dizzy. Big Ruby Mitchell gingerly touched his nose. Leroy Hipps looked down at his fingers. The rain had stopped now, and a ghostly mist rose from the black land all around us. The stalks of dead cotton stretched interminably away, and the Delta autumnal bugs began to splatter against the windshield.

The second beer was even better than the first, sending mellow waves all through me. I leaned back in my seat and gazed out at the great sweep of the land in the darkness.

At that moment, with no warning, Billy Bonner stood up from the back seat of The Choctaw, breaking the long silence.

"Well, boys," he shouted, flourishing his bottle of Jax with his undamaged hand, and everyone turned to look at the valiant little figure standing there. *"Boys, we won!* . . . We won, by God. *We won away from home in the last minute!"*

I suppose we knew, Billy and Bubba and Hershell and all of us, that Belzoni would be among our finest hours.

That Saturday night, for the midnight show at the Rebel it was *A Place in the Sun* with Liz Taylor and Montgomery Clift. Katie and I chose not to double-date with Billy Bonner and Debbie. When a couple, new to one another, was getting "serious," they would go it alone. We parked on Cemetery Hill. Do you remember, Katie? It *was* starting to get serious, wasn't it?

As for the Choctaws, we had our vicissitudes leading to the November 22 mismatch with Jackson Central. We lost to Drew the next week, 20–14, then tied Batesville 14–14 and beat West Tallahatchie 20–12. Then on consecutive Fridays at home we were trounced by Kosciusko 32–14 and Cleveland 27–7. Coach Blackie Piersall sent me into all of these games, but never for more than three or four routine plays. I carried the ball six times for a net gain of twelve yards. Billy Bonner was firmly entrenched at right halfback, Hershell Meade was the best punter in the D.V.C., and at left half, despite our ignominious record, Bubba Poindexter—six feet, 195, and ten flat in the hundred—was being touted for all-state.

The Saturday morning after the Cleveland debacle, several of us were lounging in the sunshine in the park. We had the Jackson paper. The banner headline in the sports section read:

Jackson Central Outclasses Greenville 48–0

And the smaller headline underneath:

Throwaway Game Friday
Before Vicksburg Showdown

"Throwaway game!" Billy Bonner said in disgust. He snatched the paper from Hershell Meade and perused the article. Then he read the Jackson record out loud to us. I still have that clipping. It is here before me now as I write these words, all shrivelled and yellow.

Jackson Central	48	Natchez	0
Jackson Central	34	Meridian	7
Jackson Central	53	Biloxi	12
Jackson Central	41	Tupelo	7
Jackson Central	47	Memphis Central (Tenn.)	7
Jackson Central	34	Gulfport	0
Jackson Central	55	Hattiesburg	0
Jackson Central	48	Greenville	0

Katie was lying in my lap looking up at the clouds. Debbie was painting her toenails. Bubba and Laura Jane were reading the front page of the paper about the war. Hershell was flexing his fingers where he had been stepped on the night before. In a moment Hooker, a tall colored boy who went to the Number Two High School, ambled by on the sidewalk with a lawn rake over his shoulder.

"Hey, Hooker!" Billy Bonner said. "I heard you got stomped yesterday by Durant. How come you let little ol' Durant do that?"

"Yeah," Hooker said. "I heard *you* got stomped by little ol' Cleveland. Ain't you *ashamed*?"

"We'll whip you Number Two boys any time, Hooker," Billy said.

Billy's antagonist was some distance beyond us now. "Who y'all playin' next week anyhow?" he shouted. "What's the name of that town? You needs me! You needs somebody to catch a pass, not bobble it like a egg. You got guys who can't catch a *watermelon*." And he laughed crazily.

"Can *you* catch it, Hooker?"

"Oh yeah, can I catch it! Can *you* catch it?"

Billy shouted a curse, and Hooker hooted some more, then vanished around Calhoun Street.

Something was snapping in Billy Bonner, having to do with the strain of the season, perhaps, or the challenge awaiting us next Friday, or maybe a profounder concern, although I always doubted if Billy were any different on the inside from what he was on his surface.

"That one looks like God," Katie said.

"*What* looks like God?" Billy demanded.

"That big cloud up there."

"Damn you, Katie, you're dumb."

I looked up at the cloud, and sure enough it *did* look like God, if you approached it from a certain angle.

"And what's that *book* you got there?" he asked me.

"It's a library book," I said. Billy picked it up and examined it.

It was called *The Sun Also Rises* by Ernest Hemingway.

"What's it about?" he asked.

"I don't know."

"It's got to be about something besides the sun rising," he persisted.

In truth, I was having a hard time with that book. "Well," I replied, "it's about . . . losing."

"Losing!" Billy said.

"Yeah," Hershell Meade interjected. "We're experts on that."

Billy slammed down the book and left to go squirrel hunting with his cousins in Panther Creek.

He had been gone no more than a few minutes when the funeral procession came by—one of the country boys several grades ahead of us, brought back now from Korea. The long obsidian hearse reflected the morning's sun as it led the cars slowly on its journey to the cemetery. We watched silently as the sad parade went by, then talked a little about the boy, who was only a wisp out of a distant past for us. When the last car turned left on Lamar, we got up to leave.

That afternoon Katie and I took her mother's car and, just to get out of town, drove down to Vicksburg. It was chilly and clear on the drive south over the last finger of the Delta, and the land was flooded from the rains until we reached the hills. On the radio we had the Ole Miss-Tennessee game from Memphis, then we switched to the dance music from WWL. The haunted town on the river bluffs drowsed in the autumn sun and gave an aura of age and suffering and faint riverboat decadence. We rode up and down the steep inclines past the mansions half-hidden by towering magnolias and the courthouse which had somehow survived the shellings. Out in the battlefield, we walked through the endless rows of Union gravestones. The ground was heavy with fallen leaves, the squirrels danced about everywhere, and out in the distance was the echo of a train's whistle.

We drove by the gullies and ravines and the hilly terrain dotted with the monuments to the top of the bluffs. We got out and sat on the steps and looked toward the river at the far horizon, shimmering in the November gold. I had my arm around Katie, and suddenly some Yankee tourists appeared from beyond the rampart, saying cheery hellos and leaving us to our privacy. We sat there for a long time, watching as the river turned to deep shades of brown with the sun's descent.

"What are you thinking about?" she asked.

"A lot of things . . . How much I want the season to end, I guess."

"Will you go with me next year—to Ole Miss?"

"I'll try."

"I want you with me." She looked at me with her impish green eyes.

"I know that. I want to go with you too."

A curious thing happened that next week, not unfamiliar perhaps to the human species. Even in the certainty of defeat, the town became obsessed with the Friday night game, as if pride itself, indulged before the fact, would dampen the ashes of sorrow. It was said that about half the white population would travel the sixty miles in private cars and several chartered Southern Trailways buses. The director of the band had ordered new saddle oxfords for all the musicians, assessing them five dollars apiece for this acquisition. The cheerleaders had been preparing a special set of acts for several days, to culminate in a dissolving pyramid of flesh, girls somersaulting to the ground at perfect three-second intervals. Huge hand-lettered, red-and-black signs appeared overnight all over town, sponsored by the Kiwanis Club and Fulgate's Tire Store, saying: "Go Get 'Em, Choctaws!" There was an unexpected demand for red and black crepe paper in Woolworth's and Kuhn's. Our Jewish mayor, Mr. Fred O. Fink, issued a proclamation urging support of the team "against an unnamed metropolis sixteen times larger than ours." In response to an article by the sports editor of the Jackson *Clarion-Ledger* suggesting that the scheduling of the game was a travesty and asking the cadre of Jackson Central coaches to give their regulars the night off, Billy Bonner's father wrote a personal letter telling the editor precisely where to place his column, and at what angle. On Sunday, by prearrangement, the pastors of the Baptist, Methodist, and Presbyterian churches offered prayers involving the traditions of the town and the school and the gallant and unblemished Christian allegiances of both. The Episcopalians, it was rumored, would have joined this display of strength but felt it out of character with *their* traditions, so they would charter a bus for their parishioners instead. The Boy Scout and Cub Scout troops were going en masse in

their uniforms. The Choctaw got its first washing and greasing of the season, and the local weekly, *The Sentinel*, ran a front-page headline accompanying the team picture: "Brave Little Choctaws Face Big City Boys."

If the truth be known, Katie and I met three times that week at the noontime break, skipping cafeteria, in a secret place behind the Brickyard Grove. She went out the back door of the school and walked up Filmore and Calhoun the quarter of a mile to the bayou. I left through the front door and went up Davis, taking a shortcut through several backyards to the grove. Our rendezvous was the cool secret glade of cedars by the creek, a bosky glade of my childhood.

Later, sitting on her front porch after football practice that Monday, I could have cared less about a game, even this one. I only wanted to be with Katie. She took my hand and told me the majorettes were putting small battery flashlights on each end of their batons for the game. "Isn't it exciting?" she asked. "Aren't you excited?"

"No," I said.

I felt guilty about discouraging her enthusiasm, for I would have done anything for Katie that day. But that afternoon Coach Blackie Piersall had given us a savant's description of the Jackson Central squad, which averaged 220 pounds from end to end. They had held their opponents, the aristocrats of the Mississippi gridiron, to sixteen first downs all season! They worked from a single-wing offense and were three-deep in all positions. Their entire starting team, he said, would play in college.

Coach Piersall had led us to a fetid, isolated spot under the grandstand, having chased away the three or four dozen spectators who had come out of curiosity, or masochism, to observe our preparations. "We're just coming out full-throttle," he said. "A lot of passes and pitch-outs, and leave the big line alone if possible." He went on to explain that he was installing three or four unusual new plays that he had not taught us before now because he did not think we could handle them, but that we had nothing to lose anyway. Johnny Vaught at Ole Miss had used these plays only in the direst emergency, he said. One, for instance, was a double reverse with the right halfback eventually passing all the way across the field to the left end. Another was called "Sprint Left," which was a pass play where the key man was the fullback, Big Ruby Mitchell. He brush-blocked the defensive end and slipped downfield as a receiver. The quarterback, Hershell Meade, had the option of running or throwing, depending on what the end did. If the end dropped back to cover Big Ruby, Hershell ran. If he committed to containment, Hershell threw long to Big Ruby.

"This is a dandy play," Blackie Piersall said. "But I ain't sure you're up to it. What the hell? We'll try it. Anyhow, you can't use it but once."

"Above all," he shouted under the grandstand that day, "hold your heads high! And remember Belzoni! And don't read the damned Jackson papers!"

There was, in fact, a wonderfully infectious spirit to the practices later that week—not unlike, I imagined, the Japanese kamikazi pilots I had read about from World War II, and the ceremonies they had before they took off in their Zeroes.

On Thursday, Principal Buffaloe came on the loudspeaker. "Because we want you to get to Jackson for the game early tomorrow evening," he said, "and not have to rush too much and get all reckless, school will be dismissed at noon." The rest of his remarks, which invoked the Lord, went unheeded before the cheers and claps and whistles which reverberated through the old building from every classroom, a wild and reckless incantation that could have been heard in the fishing boats on the river.

Friday came, and it was cold. A frigid wind had sprung up from the Delta. The sky was a hard, brittle blue.

We went through the ritual of morning classes. Mrs. Idella King read to us from Tennyson:

> "Though much is taken, much abides;
> One equal temper of heroic hearts,
> Made weak by time and fate, but strong in will
> To strive, to seek, to find, and not to yield

I was following the words from the textbook, and I noticed she left out the following lines after "abides":

> and though
> We are not that strength which in old days
> Moved earth and heaven, that which we are, we are—

Moments after the noon bell, the school was strangely deserted, except for the band, which tarried to practice Sousa marches from its quarters in a reconverted Quonset hut behind the school, and the majorettes, who were rehearsing their routines outdoors to the tune of the marches. Blackie Piersall had gotten the managers to lay out pallets on the basketball court so we could rest in the early afternoon. Many of the team dozed there in their sock feet, and Big Ruby Mitchell snored horrendously through his broken nose from the

Belzoni game. Others stretched out and talked in nervous whispers. Coach Piersall, who had been helping the managers load the uniforms, came into the gymnasium and everyone was quiet again. Then he went back outside.

Ed Wilburn Walters, on the next pallet, nudged Billy Bonner and me and pointed to the large set of windows at the far end of the court. There was Debbie, who had climbed onto something to reach the high window outside and was waving in to Billy, and Billy waved back. Momentarily Laura Jane appeared there and waved at Bubba Poindexter. When she vanished, my heart skipped a throb, for my heart was telling me who would be there next, and there she was, Katie, so pert and lovely and I had to take a deep breath as she smiled at me through the glass. Then she too was gone.

Blackie Piersall shouted at us to get up and put on our shoes. On a blackboard in the center of the basketball court he stressed the important Jackson Central offensive plays again. Next, for the twentieth time, he diagrammed the new plays he had installed for us.

Then we were off in The Choctaw, stopping at the Tenderloin Grill again for the roast beef and mashed potatoes, and heading now up and down the hills covered with seared kudzu, through the sleepy impoverished little Mississippi hamlets in the chilled sunshine toward our appointment. Cars with red-and-black streamers sped past, blowing their horns, and the passengers waved enthusiastically. The chartered bus filled with the Boy Scouts roared by, and they let down their windows and cheered, their driver sounding the bus horn to the exact beat of the fight song. Soon the bus carrying the band slipped in behind us and blew *its* horn, and it stayed right there all the way, as a cruiser might escort a stricken destroyer to port. I knew Katie was back there somewhere.

The shadows of late autumn fell on the forlorn hills, and the trees and even the telephone poles covered with the creeping kudzu were tossed in grotesque silhouettes. In the outlying town of Pocahontas the street lights were already on. Then we rounded a bend and were at the outskirts of the immense city which Sherman had burned years and years ago, and which had risen up again long before we were born and was waiting for us now.

Far in the distance the state capitol loomed before us, illuminated with floodlights, like a picture postcard against the darkening sky.

There are some things which come back in memory as in a dream. Psychiatry reminds us that dreams tell us who we are. I myself have learned that many of

the ineffable moments of life—moments of grief or ecstasy or suffering, of love or triumph or sorrow—are dream-like in their unfolding, at once softer and more stark than reality itself.

So it was for me that night in the big stadium off State Street. What was it but a dream?

I remember the deafening noise from the crowd as we lined up at the entranceway under the stadium. We wore black jerseys with white numerals, and black-and-red pants and helmets. The halfbacks and ends wore low-quarter shoes, the linemen full-quarter ones, and our cleats rattled on the concrete as we waited there, jumping up and down to keep warm. I looked down at my jersey, Number 22, and across at Bubba Poindexter's, Number 24, and for no reason at all I recalled my first memory of Bubba. We were four years old and I was killing ants with a hammer on the sidewalk in front of my house, and Bubba said: "The Lord ain't goin' to like that." Now, wordlessly, Bubba and I bumped our shoulder pads together to get them straight.

Then, on Blackie Piersall's signal, we rushed through the entranceway onto the opulent green field. The cheers from our townspeople seemed pathetic in the vast structure, so horrifically outnumbered by the thousands of Jackson Central partisans, and our band was as reedy and off-key as it had always been. An eerie autumnal half-moon had ascended out beyond the field lights, and when the Jackson Central squad appeared from the opposite end of the stadium, big and swift and menacing in their flashy black-and-gold, the roar from the stands and the brassy beat of the prodigious band and the yells of three or four dozen cheerleaders who led them out and the explosion of a small cannon in their end zone made one's very footfalls on the grass of the turf inaudible. There truly were about seventy-five of them, and under the giddy beams of light with the stands rising high into the night they seemed of sufficient numbers to have overrun McClellan at Sharpsburg.

Soon Bubba Poindexter and Hershell Meade were at midfield shaking hands with the Jackson captains—one of them a lineman of at least six and a half feet—and Bubba and Hershell ran back to the rest of us waiting in a semicircle in front of our bench. We had won the toss of the coin and would receive from the north goal. We gathered around Blackie Piersall and recited the Lord's Prayer, and then stood at attention for "The Star-Spangled Banner." When that was over our band began the fight song, but no sooner had they played three or four bars than the Jackson band drowned them out with theirs.

In the course of human events, as all mystics comprehend, there can be a magic, defying all logic, which will seize a moment, something absurd and indeed existential, undergirded by old unfathomable mysteries—the eternal enigmas of the Old Testament, for instance—and this, of course, is the material of poets. On that faraway night, in the instant the Jackson kicker let fly his long end-over-end kick, there had to be a poet's soul in Bubba Poindexter as he stood waiting on our 5-yard line.

Bubba took the ball in his chest and moved swiftly to the left side, then slowed ever so briefly to watch the lay of the blocking. Of this there was practically none. The Jackson defense was speeding down in his direction like behemoths, knocking over the entire left flank of our kickoff phalanx, and in one startling moment Bubba turned at a complete angle on the 15-yard line and reversed his field, making a rounded arc in the wrong direction as he did so. One Jackson player hit him on the ankle on the 25 and he stumbled before regaining his balance, but miraculously the whole right side of the field opened up with the exception of a mammoth end who was rushing in to cut Bubba off near the sidelines. From nowhere came Leroy Hipps, who chopped the end to earth with a jarring block.

That was all there was to it. Bubba sped by me only a yard or two away on the bench—I could have reached out and touched his jersey—staying just inside the boundary, the entire gridiron empty before him. When he reached the opposite end zone, there was not a Jackson player within twenty-five yards. A few seconds after that, Hershell Meade split the uprights for the extra point.

The human animal needs time to digest experience. It had all happened too fast, consuming about as many seconds as it may have taken the reader to read the previous two paragraphs. Even our own players did not respond precipitously to Bubba's ninety-five-yard touchdown. Two or three of them may have slapped him on the back as they returned to the huddle for Hershell Meade's extra point, but there were no shouts or wild embracings. In fact, when Bubba crossed their goal, the Jackson thousands seemed still to be cheering from the adrenalin of the opening kickoff, and our outnumbered loyalists desperately needed a moment or two to absorb that to which they had just been witness. By the time of Hershell's conversion, however, a silence impenetrable as mortal death had settled upon the Jacksonians while our students and townspeople, so indiscriminately crowded in the lower seats behind our bench, sent forth a terrific roar that would have frightened hearty attack dogs away, and began hugging one another as if their lives depended on it.

Jackson Central made two quick first downs after the ensuing kickoff, and then ground to a halt. Something enigmatic was transpiring in the interior line. Unbelievable as it may seem, our linemen were fighting them down, clawing them down like beasts fighting for survival. Outweighed thirty pounds to the man, Leroy Hipps and Big Boy Hendrix and the others were not merely standing their ground, they were penetrating that horrendous single-wing blocking, bleeding and cursing and gang-tackling, and opening tiny crevices on offense for Bubba Poindexter and Billy Bonner and Big Ruby Mitchell to squirm through. On a third and twenty Bubba gained twenty-eight yards on one of Blackie Piersall's new secret plays. Big Ruby got fourteen on another new play. But these were the only substantial gains for either side, and at the end of the first quarter, the score stood 7–0.

Time passed swiftly in the second period. Neither team could move the ball consistently, and that enigmatic game settled down into exchanges of fourth-down punts. I had known Hershell Meade since he first started kicking footballs in the second grade, and he had never kicked better. The vicious, crushing action largely was taking place between the two 30-yard lines.

A mounting tension suffused the atmosphere, not orgiastic now, but a subtle deepening of emotion. We were holding them! Billy Bonner even intercepted one of their passes on our 40-yard line in that quarter, and Cotton Simmons burst through later and threw the Jackson tailback, fading for a pass, for an eighteen-yard loss. Unaccustomed to such peremptory treatment, the Jackson players resorted to venomous oaths and taunts. Two fistfights erupted, and Hans Weems was penalized fifteen yards for hitting his opposite number with clenched fists after his adversary had elbowed him in the groin, the original transgression having been missed by the referees. Our foe was also having difficulties with penalties, on one late hit and three clips. Given the ferocity of play at the line, it was surprising there were no serious injuries. Big Ruby Mitchell lost a tooth to go with his broken nose, Kayo Fentress sustained a gash on his forearm, Cotton Simmons had an index finger dislocated, and Hershell Meade had to come out for two plays feeling giddy, but when he realized he was on the sidelines, he ran back into the fray without so much as conferring with Blackie Piersall.

Patently it was the element of surprise which was making the Jackson Central team so sluggish. Had they played the role of Mississippi bully for too many seasons? Near the end of the first half, when their tailback was crushed out of bounds on their 28-yard-line by Leroy Hipps and Hans Weems for a six-yard loss and three or four of their players came to help him to his feet, from my spot on the bench I saw the expression of astonishment in their eyes. Not hurt, only incredulity, the way General Hooker must have looked at Chancellorsville when he gazed to his rear and sighted Stonewall's emaciated, barefoot infantrymen coming up fast. I knew enough football, too, to perceive that Blackie Piersall was relying now on his innate conservatism. With notable exceptions, little of the histrionic action he had said we would need had been summoned. The second quarter, as with most of the first, was a matter of pitiless bone-crushing.

A funny emotion had seized certain sections of the big stadium. With two minutes remaining in the half, I looked around and noticed that more and more people here and there were cheering our team. At first I was baffled by this phenomenon, but then I perceived what it was. The hundreds of small-town people who had come to observe the unchallengeable Jacksonians were reverting to their origins. They sensed a historic vengeance. They were with us.

I heard a yell from the back of the bench. The band was coming down for its halftime performance. There was Katie, shivering in her tight majorette's uniform, the flashlights twinkling on each end of her baton. "Isn't it wonderful?" she shouted; then she vanished in the throng.

Soon the gun sounded for the first half, with us in possession on our own 31-yard line. The score was 7–0.

Blackie Piersall was uncharacteristically subdued in the locker room at halftime, in fact almost a benign presence, going over some of the enemy's favorite offensive plays and defensive alignments on the blackboard, and the team was as quiet as he, resting for the mighty drama ahead. Coach Piersall's only concession to the accumulating tension came when we got up to leave. "Just remember," he said. "You can tell your grandchildren about this!"

The third quarter began as the second had ended, unspectacular exchanges between the 30-yard lines, small gains, and fourth-down punts. As the minutes ticked by, however, I saw that our opponents' coaches were beginning to dispatch more and more substitutes from their untapped reservoir of manpower. I overheard Blackie Piersall whispering to Dr. Tommy Gilruth: "They're gonna try to wear us down."

There were two minutes, forty-seven seconds left in the third quarter and we had a first and ten from our own 29 when it finally happened. Billy Bonner took a pitchout from Hershell Meade and was skirting left-end when two Jackson linemen upended him with an agonizing tackle which could be heard all the way across the field.

Billy did not get up.

Blackie Piersall and Dr. Tommy Gilruth rushed out and bent over Billy Bonner. They stayed there a long time. Bubba Poindexter and Big Ruby Mitchell helped him off the field. Already his ankle was swollen to twice its size. "For Christ's sake, don't touch the damned thing," Billy cried as they laid him out behind the bench.

The moment had come, as I knew it might, as if my entire seventeen years had been building toward it. Blackie Piersall called my name. I went over to him as I strapped on my helmet, walking as calmly as I could to disguise the dreadful turmoil inside.

"Just take it easy," he said. "Tell Hershell 68-B left. We'll start you right off." Sixty-eight-B left was the right halfback's call.

Need it be said that what one sees on the field is a world apart from the bench? The hatred in the eyes of the enemy linemen, the whispered threats, the falsetto squeals of pain, the fatigue etched deeply in the faces of one's teammates were larger than mere life. The dream had taken over again.

Sixty-eight-B was a quarterback pitchout with the right halfback sweeping wide to the left. Before I knew it, Hershell Meade had faked to Big Red Ruby at fullback and then the pitch was coming out to me. I took it at a canter and followed two blockers. Suddenly the broad swathe of daylight which had appeared in the left-flat closed. Three huge Jackson defenders attacked from all sides. I fell with a crash to the soft earth. When I got up I felt numb, yet all the nervousness had dissolved. I had gained seven yards!

Gene Autry Simms ran in from the sidelines to the huddle. "S-s-same play!" he ordered. "S-s-same damned p-p-play!" This time I took the lateral from much farther out. Hershell's aim was not as accurate as before, but I had it at the knees. The whole left side of our line was holding off the front defenders. There was a large opening now off to the center, and beyond that, where the linebackers were being staggered by fierce blocks, another empty space flickered in the corner of my eye. I moved in that direction, picking up speed as I ran. An enemy defensive back was closing in from the left, but Hans Weems appeared before me to brush him aside, and I was momentarily free, moving easily and alone as in the races we once had at recess in grammar school. Out of the old inexplicable instincts of one born to run fast I cut toward the left sidelines, until another defensive back struck me from the right, and I kept going until I stumbled out of bounds. I got up again and looked around. We were on their 33-yard line. I had gained thirty-two yards.

Blackie Piersall was sending in every play now. Bubba on the quick-opener

for three. Big Ruby on a trap for one. Bubba on a pitchout for one. The third quarter ended with us on their 30-yard line, fourth down and five to go.

We went to the opposite end of the field for the huddle. Gene Autry galloped in again. "S-s-seventy-four-B extra s-s-special," he said.

"Again?" Hershell Meade asked him.

"S-s-seventy-four-B extra s-s-special."

"Are you sure?" Hershell persisted.

"F-f-fuckin'-A, I'm sure," Gene Autry said. "Y-y-you think I'd s-s-screw up now?"

Seventy-four-B extra special was one of the new plays, the double-reverse with the right halfback finally getting the ball, stopping in his tracks on the far left side and passing all the way across the field to the end deep. We had practiced it all week.

"Can you handle it?" Hershell asked me.

"I'll try," I said.

We moved from the huddle. Then the play began to unfold, Bubba Poindexter shoving the football squarely into my stomach as I dashed to the right. I stopped. Two tacklers were heading toward me. As I gazed downfield, everything seemed to move in slow, unhurried, exaggerated motions, belabored, surrealistic and blurred. I even remember seeing the eerie half-moon, and under it, all alone and waving frantically to me, gyrating all over like a man in the throes of seizure was my friend from kindergarten on—Ed Wilburn Walters, the number on his jersey, 88, standing out sharp and clear as a vision. I cocked my arm and threw the ball in his direction, farther it seemed than I had ever thrown anything in my life, so that my whole right arm tingled with the effort, the way one feels when he hits his funny bone on the edge of a hard object, and at that instant the two tacklers plummeted into me, and I crashed again to the ground. A few seconds later, one of the Jackson tacklers, who was still half-sitting on me, said: "Shit!"

By the time I was upright, Bubba Poindexter raced over and pounded me on the back. So did Hershell and Big Ruby. A fervid din rose from our spectators.

"What happened?" I asked.

"He caught it, you fool!" Bubba said. "Right on the goal line. Only end-over-end pass I ever saw."

Hershell's kick was perfect once more, and we led 14–0 with fourteen minutes, forty-two seconds left in the game.

Blackie Piersall would not use me on defense. Instead he put Hans Weems in the defensive backfield where Billy Bonner had been. As I sat there again on the bench, I understood now what our coach had meant about the enemy's reserves. There was a whole new group on almost every play. As for us, the ceaseless pounding without relief was beginning to wreak its toll. Our players moved slowly after every play.

This draconian fatigue showed when the enemy's second-team offense gradually moved upfield after our kickoff. Wide gaps in our defense elicited runs of twenty, fourteen, and seventeen yards, and a screen-pass went for twelve. With 10:41 to play, as if an afterthought, they scored on a post-pattern from our 11-yard line, adding the point to make it 14–7.

In the huddle when our turn came, there were groans and laborious breathing. "Them bastards are dirty as Belzoni," Leroy Hipps said. Yet we managed two first downs, the second coming on a five-yard gain by me to our own 44. On a fourth and eight from our 48, Hans Weems replaced me, and I watched from the bench as Hershell Meade booted a long, true spiral to the Jackson 7. One of their vast corps of halfbacks gathered in the ball and started upfield. Our bench cried in misery as he broke open on his 30. Cotton Simmons, the only man between him and the goal, succeeded in bringing him down on our 34. Seven plays later they scored on a short pass into the flat. They kicked the point.

The score was 14–14 with 5:36 left to play.

Again we could not move the ball. I was thrown for a four-yard loss on the same 68-B which had succeeded earlier. Big Ruby Mitchell was stopped for no gain. Bubba Poindexter took a short pass from Hershell Meade and sprang free for seventeen yards to our 43-yard line. But that was all. With 4:20 to go, the intrepid Hershell Meade kicked out of bounds on the enemy's 12-yard line.

From the bench I heard now a sound unlike any I had ever heard before, a vast rhythmic roar, filling the Mississippi night under its stark November half-moon. It had an unearthly resonance, cruel and smug and old as time, an unholy incantation against all of us who have ever been outnumbered, and tired, and in pain, and a long way from home. "*Go . . . Go . . . Go . . . Go . . . !*" The thousands of Jackson partisans were standing, stretching their arms and gesturing in unison, encouraged by the slow, erotic beat of their drums and cymbals, and the yells of their many women, and the echo of their momentous chant resounded off the facades of both sides of the stadium and merged on the field where we stood. "*Go . . . Go . . . Go . . . Go . . . !*"

Our foe marched from the huddle. Four up the middle. Seven on a buttonhook. Six on a power right. Nine on a power left. Five on a buttonhook. Eleven on a screen pass. The big scoreboard showed one minute, fifty-nine seconds left in the game and Jackson had a first and ten on our 47-yard line. They were moving now, and they knew it, with their fresh, undirtied recruits, bludgeoning our line, riddling our secondary with short swift passes.

The Jackson tailback faded for another pass. Far downfield, behind Hans Weems, one of their ends was breaking clear. The tailback poised to throw. As he did so, in the pristine moment of throwing long, Leroy Hipps crashed through two blockers and brushed the tailback's shoulder. The ball hovered for a moment in mid-air, just beyond the line of scrimmage, wobbling like a dying bird in flight, and as it fell earthward Ed Wilburn Walters with one prodigious effort swooped toward it, embracing it with both arms in a passionate gesture of belonging. Then he fell to the turf. At first we could not see, because his back was to us, but the referees made their motions and everyone helped Ed Wilburn to his feet.

He had intercepted the ball on our 46-yard line. One minute, forty-eight seconds to play.

Everything came swifter now, in a prism of tangled bodies and brute flailings. Big Ruby for seven to the Jackson 47. Bubba Poindexter for six and the first down on the Jackson 41. "Belzoni!" Bubba whispered in the huddle. Then, almost tenderly: *"Remember Belzoni?"*

"Sprint Left," the last new play, came in from the bench. Big Ruby Mitchell would slip deep downfield, Hershell Meade having the option of running or throwing, depending on what big Number 86, the defensive end, did. Hershell took the snap and dashed to the left, eluding a throng of tacklers, then against every dictum in the book, faded back. It was almost a failed play. He heaved. Lying prone on the ground, I peered through the night. Big Ruby Mitchell leapt higher and higher, far over the torso of a lone defender. He came down with the ball on the 7-yard line.

One minute even remained, as we called time-out and gathered in the huddle. Everyone was gasping for air. Blood streamed out of the sleeve of my jersey. Hershell Meade had a nasty, battered eye. Leroy Hipps had a jagged cut under his nose. Bubba Poindexter stared across at me without expression. The stadium was now ghostly silent, like a sepulcher. An insane thought ran through my brain, from my readings in Mrs. Idella King's class. Someone would dig this all up someday and surmise: there seemed to have been a public meeting place here.

Gene Autry Simms interrupted my demented reverie. "Forty-two-A." It was Bubba Poindexter's call, the standard Split-T quick-opener up the middle.

In the Split-T, it must be said here, which was perfected by Don Faurot at

Missouri and refined by Bud Wilkinson at Oklahoma and Johnny Vaught at Ole Miss in the late 1940s (and became long-since outmoded) the fullback lined up directly behind the quarterback three yards deep. The left- and right-halfbacks were positioned on either side of the fullback, also three yards deep. On the quick-opener, at the snap of the ball from the center to the quarterback, or on the signal for the snap—*Ready* or *Set* or *One* or *Two* or *Three* or *Four*—the two halfbacks would sprint straight out of their pointed stance for the line of scrimmage. In our lexicon, on "42-A" the quarterback would hand off to the left halfback heading directly toward the middle of the opposing line, crashing through it behind quick, precise blocking. On "42-B" the hand-off was to the right halfback on exactly the same pattern.

Now we are in the huddle. Hershell crouches before us. *"Forty-two-A—Off on Set."* We go to the line. Hershell bends behind Big Boy Hendrix at center. Now he shouts: "Ready . . . *Set!*" The play develops with breathless precision. Bubba batters through the enemy line for three yards, to the 4-yard line.

Fifty seconds.

Once more we are in the huddle. Cotton Simmons comes in from the bench and is standing before us. "Forty-two-B."

"Again?" I ask.

"Forty-two-B."

And Hershell: *"Forty-two-B . . . Off on One."*

We break the huddle, taking the familiar pointed stance. Is anything what it ever seems to be? There is one final, all-meaning silence as Hershell kneels behind the center. Then: "Ready . . . Set . . . *One!*"

I hurdle ahead, feeling the whack in my abdomen. For the merest instant I feel the clawing of desperate boys, the hammer of big adolescent bodies, and then as I pitch forward a terrible blow to my midriff spins me off-course, and I am plummeting downward into an abyss of flesh.

Only when I hit the earth do I sense I am no longer holding the ball. It is bouncing crazily to my right, out of the range of the manswarm which entraps me. I reach helplessly for it, reach out very far, but it is gone from me, irretrievably and forever. As it settles on the 1-yard line, just before the enemy end pounces lovingly upon it, I see the contrast between the brown of the ball and the deep green of the grass.

I awakened in my bed the next morning to the memory of it. People were not as bad as they could have been. After all, some of them volunteered, we tied Central High of Jackson.

But I saw it in their eyes. Some of my comrades avoided me in the dressing room. Leroy Hipps shook his head when he saw me. Blackie Piersall patted me on the back and went on with his duties, but his eyes were unforgiving. One of the Jackson coaches, who had come over to shake hands with Blackie Piersall, bent down with a whiskey breath and whispered, "Thanks, kid." Some of our townspeople, waiting outside as we walked to The Choctaw, turned away as I passed.

She was waiting for me, Katie, in a little circle of shadows near The Choctaw. I could tell she had been waiting for me there in the cold for a long time. She embraced me. "My poor sweet boy," she whispered as she held me. "Did they hurt you?"

I could sense the look. When I went to see Billy Bonner in the hospital, I could tell even he was not saying what he wanted to say. Hershell and Bubba were with me in Billy's room, and Hershell said he did not remember a thing after the blow he got on his head in the second quarter. "I didn't know nothin' until . . . you know." Then he turned to me. "Hey, I'm sorry. I shouldn't have said that." I would walk up unannounced to a group of people, and there would be awkward silences. The men in the barber shop were not themselves when I came in.

It was Katie who got me through the next few days.

One afternoon a month later, however, a still weekday afternoon with no one about, I was walking down the deserted main street on an errand from school for Mrs. Idella King. Suddenly, from far behind me, I heard the word boom out at me:

"Butterfingers!"

I whirled around. There was no one in sight.

At the high school graduation that May, when Principal Buffaloe handed me my diploma and announced I had beaten Marion Whittington by two-tenths of a grade-point and was the valedictorian, he looked at the audience in the gymnasium, where we had rested on pallets that day before driving to Jackson, and added: "So you see, we forgive him his little . . . *mistake*." Everyone laughed and applauded.

One hot day in late August I went to say goodby to Katie, who was leaving for Ole Miss. It was the last time I ever saw her.

"I'll always love you," she said. "I'll see you Christmas."

"Christmas," I repeated.

"I'll forgive you not going with me. Didn't I adore you even after the . . . ?" She paused.

"Fumble!"

"But, my baby," she said, leaning into me as she always would, smiling at me with her sparkling green eyes. "After all, it's only a game."

That's what they always say. Even Katie—God bless my precious Katie—did not believe it. Not in that place, and in that time. Up there on the gold-paved streets of heaven, with free Dr. Peppers and strawberry milkshakes running perpetually out of the very water taps, she is looking down at me. She is whispering to me. What is it, my Katie? Speak to me before you fade from me forever, speak to the long-ago boy who loved you. I strain now to hear her words. . . "My poor sweet butterfingers."